WHEN
ISLA
MEETS
♥♥♥ LUKE
MEETS
ISLA

RHIAN TRACEY

BLOOMSBURY

For my husband Christopher,
Mam and Dad, Andrew and
Sanna for all your love,
support and encouragement

First published in Great Britain in 2003 by Bloomsbury Publishing Plc
38 Soho Square, London, W1D 3HB

A CIP catalogue record of this book is available from the British Library

ISBN 0 7475 6344 6

Printed in Great Britain by Clays Ltd, St Ives plc

1 3 5 7 9 10 8 6 4 2

ISLA

I jumped up an' down when they first told me. Finally, I would be away from the evil clutches of Baba Yaga, or Emily MacDonald as everyone else called her. We had done myths an' legends at school, an' the usual drivel about the wee ghostie girl who haunts Mary King's Close, a street they closed off in Edinburgh during the plague. Apparently, all the people who lived in the close were shut off down there, infected an' contaminated an' left to die when their close was bricked up. So in a kitchen there is the ghost of a wee girl who cries for her dolly. Then o'course there was Nessie. We went on a day trip all the way up to Inverness; it took hours on the coach. Nessie has existed since the seventh century according to our history teacher Mr Magee. I asked, 'Wouldn't she be dead by now, sir?' an' he raised his eyebrows – which are wiry, out of control, an' available in a range of colours – an' tutted at me. Now is that no' a fair question or what?

Anyway, one myth was about Baba Yaga, the original witch who ate human flesh an' lived in a hut in Russia made out of the flesh of humans. Well, whatever flesh was left over after she'd feasted on the bodies, usually leaving only their bones and skulls. Mr Magee said witches are fearful an' unnatural women, an' when he asked for an example of a modern day equivalent, I volunteered the most obvious candidate, 'Emily MacDonald?'

Mr Magee's eyebrows didn't merely raise when I nominated this contender. Instead, they performed an involuntary jig, leaning in towards one another above the cross look on the rest of his despairing face as he said ma name three times, his tone echoing the look on his face.

'Isla, Isla, Isla!'

I looked across the history room at Emily, an' her cold steely eyes informed me I ought to go and arrange ma funeral, now. Well, she wouldna be able to get me anymore.

Normally, I would have been excited about flying, no' like her on a broom but on a real plane: Flight BA 1829 from Edinburgh to Heathrow.

I could see the Forth Bridge, ma favourite red rail bridge and the blue Firth of Forth waters beneath.

The bridge's name always confuses tourists, as the other one, the road bridge, is called the Third Bridge, an' everyone always asks where the Fifth Bridge is. There isn't one. I realised I was rambling in ma head. I didna really want to leave Scotland. I wanted to have a red emergency button to press like they have on trains, to stop them, but you have to pay a fifty-pound fine if you didna have a good reason for pressing it. I did. I wanted to make the pilot turn the plane around. I wanted to go back to ma old school. I would be in S3, doing ma Standard Grade with Mr Magee, not GCSEs in some new school. I didna even know what Maidstone looked like. It sounded grey. Grey, dull and dreary. No music, no castle, no Pentland Hills, no Firth of Forth, no Lucy, no Helen, no Saturday trips into Princes Street on the bus for £1.00, except we got on for half.

I folded ma arms, an' arranged ma face into a permanent sulk with a clear *No entry* sign on it for them. 'Them' being ma parents, who have now become 'them' or 'they', as in: 'They are making me go to England' or 'Hannah and I are moving to Maidstone because of them'. Something like, ma dad had to do ma Gran's job, at the Post Office and shop, because she's ill an' would have to go into a home otherwise. I asked ma mum, 'What's wrong with homes then?' She did the Mr Magee thing of raising her eyebrows, which are definitely not wiry or colourful. Hers are neatly curved over her blue eyes an' are kept tidy with a vicious torture device she claims is a tweezer. It seems you can actually buy these instruments legally, an' inflict this painful ritual of agony upon yourself, which causes your eyes to stream an' your eyebrows, or what's left of them, to turn an attractive shade of strawberry. Anyway, ma mum didn't tut or suck air through her teeth like Mr Magee but she did say ma name three times, making it sound worse each time – 'Isla, Isla, Islaaa!' – whilst accompanying her serious expression with a slow shaking of her head.

I had hated Emily MacDonald an' knew the only way to be rid of her was to do something drastic – like kill her; or maybe move to England an' save myself from life imprisonment since I wasna really up for the whole murder thing. Despite all this, I was still no' sure about the prospect of moving countries, actually leaving Scotland an' moving to England, to Maidstone, a place I had never even heard of, which meant it was going to be *so* boring.

The thing was, in Edinburgh I had all ma friends sorted out. I had ma drama lessons with Mr James every Tuesday an' Thursday, me an' ma mates, all fourteen of us girls in one drama group an' it was the best. In the beginning, the teacher didna know what had hit him, especially on his first day in his new suit an' tie. He was really young an' pale looking, an' a wee bit geeky, not the stud we had all been hoping for but, still, he was nice an' once we'd trained him up and explained how the lessons were to go, he was sorted, an' dropped the pinstripe suit for combat trousers an' a T-shirt, thank God! We hated 'the suits' at school. They thought 'cos they were wearing one we'd automatically repect them or something. The young teachers always wore suits at first to try an' make themselves look older. It never worked – they always looked like they'd borrowed their parents' clothes. Embarrassing really.

However, the real problem was I should have had the next two years with him an' all the girls, an' now there would be all of them carrying on an' me gone. Thirteen of them left an' they said it was an ill omen that I was leaving. I didna believe in all that black magic superstition stuff but, still, I felt bad leaving them with an unlucky number. But I had no say in ma future – obviously, I was no' worthy to make decisions that would undoubtedly affect the rest of ma

9

miserable life – so why should I bother ma parents with something so unimportant as ma happiness!

If I were sixteen I could have done what I wanted, an' stayed in Edinburgh with ma cousins, an' got a job on the Royal Mile entertaining tourists, an' made a fortune no doubt.

Another thing that bothered me was I had just got ma room in order, with ma posters all on the back wall behind ma bed an' the colours on the other walls just right – three different shades of lilac and purply-lavender that I'd picked out last year in trip after trip to B & Q with the parents.

I'd just moved the furniture around as well. I liked to make it look different every now an' then to stop it from getting boring. Then I would invite ma parents and Hannah in, for a limited amount of time obviously, just to quickly observe the makeover, a wee bit like that TV programme *Changing Rooms* but without the annoying smiley presenter, an' the flirty giggle she does with Handy Andy. Ma dad says there's a reason he's called 'handy' an' it's no' to do with DIY.

I'd always try an' make it look like an adult's room, like a bedsit or a studio flat or something, like I'd seen in a magazine. It was definitely no' a kid's bedroom but all that effort an' time an' design would be for whoever had bought our house. Some other lassie would take the credit for ma colour scheme or, worse, some lad would paint it black an' put up *Star Wars* posters!

I'd hated it when people came to look at our house with all our things out on display, like embarrassing family photos, an' I could see kids who'd come with their parents to look around, sneering an' laughing at a picture of me an' Hannah. Why ma mum had to get it blown up so big I don't know – showing ma naff hairstyle with the wonky fringe. Oh, the shame!

I used to hide in ma bedroom knowing they would eventually come in an' look at all ma stuff an' ma mum would try an' make things better by knocking on ma door first, an' asking could they come in an' have a 'quick look round'. As if I could say no. So, I didna reply an' hoped they would go away, but they never did. I would suddenly have this family of four crammed into ma bedroom – strangers, people I didna know an' would never see again – commenting on the smallness of ma room or the strange colours. So sorry I couldna accommodate them better, an' that ma room wasna to their taste. The cheek!

So, now I had to leave it all behind, after all the effort I'd put into getting to know the alleyways around our road, working out the shortcuts to school an' keeping them from everyone else. All gone to waste now, left behind, just like ma life.

Then it hit me . . . I'd be the new girl, a no one. I'd have to start all over again in Maidstone an' no one would be able to say, 'I knew you'd do that', with a sense of familiarity, or, 'You're ma best mate', or anything at all really. Maybe no one would speak to me. They'd all have their friends sorted by now and there'd be no room for me. I wouldna know about the time in Year 8 when Miss so-and-so did this, or the time when this or that happened, because I wouldna have been there.

I'd seen what happens to new kids. They're whispered about and given nicknames an' no one wants the job that teachers seem to think is such a privilege – the job of being their 'friend' for the week an' showing them around the school, an' walking them to their lessons, even when you don't want to. You canny talk with your mates openly in case the new person is a geek or a grass an' you have to lie to them an' tell them all about the teachers an' the rules an' really show off about all you know, on your turf.

I would be on the other side now, I would be on the receiving end of all this, all that I had done before, no longer the confident one in ma own little world. I'd be back to square one, back at the bottom of the pile, the new girl, the Scottish girl with a weird name. I hated ma parents for that an' they had no idea.

So we flew to the south of England three weeks after they told Hannah an' me in the quiet of the lounge with the TV off – always a clear sign of bad news or a serious telling-off.

On the plane I watched ma mum smiling politely at everyone, ma dad frantically typing vital statistics into his laptop, an' Hannah playing on her Gameboy with no real appreciation of what the flight meant. Being in primary school she hadn't worked it out yet. And me, I was chewing ma lip and fidgeting whilst trying no' to punch the hostess – sorry, stewardess – who asked me three times if I was excited.

LUKE

'Mum! Where's my *Tricolore 4*? Mum? I put it on the table and now it's gone. Why can't you tidy underneath the book and then put it back? This isn't an ideal home exhibition. People have to live in this house and people make mess.'

I was getting in a state. No doubt about it. My own fault. I should have sorted it last night but *Scream 3* was on the floor in Matthew's room. He was down the pub and his battered old video was empty – what would any normal person have done? So now I know why L'Oreal think the divine Courtney Cox Arquette is 'worth it', and I have to agree, but now I can't find my heavy, musty, covered-in-old-wallpaper French book, customised by its previous owner with several drawings of breasts and the compulsory swear words. I know my French teacher Madame Bouviere will not understand the altar of Courtney and that she has priority over *Tricolore* French books. Now, if they had pictures of any of the lovely ladies from *Friends* in them I would feel obliged to take French a bit more seriously. As it is I have no interest in Monsieur Baker and his family.

No doubt my mum has obsessively tidied it away, as she seems to be in training for 'Mum of the Year' award due to take place at this year's Ideal Homes exhibition – which is where my mum can be found camping out for most of the summer, the saddo. I find her sitting at the table, calmly pouring skimmed, 'I'm-so-healthy', milk into her flowery mug of tea, whilst writing her class reports. Teachers! We all know this 'skimmed milk' pretence is really blue water coloured to con the dieting masses and those who like to think they are adopting a healthy eating attitude, as they cram themselves with chocolate croissants, which they allow themselves because they drink skimmed milk. It's like ordering a Big Mac and fries, then a Diet Coke to make it better. Will they ever learn? My mum says my teenage metabolism will only last until I am thirty and then I will suddenly have to eat the amounts normal human beings eat. I can't see this happening but I think the thought keeps her going as she eats her whole week's quota of Weight Watchers' diet biscuits in ten seconds.

Anyway, if it was her lesson I'd lost a book for, she'd

be searching and shouting and yelling stuff at me, like how I need to take responsibility for myself now I am in Year 10 and taking GCSEs, GCSEs, GCSEs. Like Tony Blair, my mum, also known as Mrs Field, likes to repeat herself. Just my luck that she, like the prime minister, is into education, education, education – mainly mine! She picks up her paper and annoyingly begins humming the French national anthem whilst trying, unsuccessfully, not to laugh.

'What?'

I am not amused. I am late. I am hungry and tired and losing the will to live over the whole missing-in-action French book. If Madame Bouviere wasn't such a candidate for the menopause or sanity testing I wouldn't care, but to be honest she really is quite terrifying when she's mid hot flush. This is what comes of living with your mum and not your dad, you find out far too much about women, especially middle-aged women.

Mum finally takes pity and decides to help me.

'Underneath my paper?'

She looks down at the table where my stupid French book is covered with her boring, impossible newspaper *The Times*, which you can't read unless you lie down on the floor, I tried it once. My mum doesn't lie down on the floor, she obviously came equipped with skills we lesser mortals don't have. I stroppily shove the book into my carefully battered-looking rucksack which narrowly escaped being washed by my mum! As if I could turn up for school with a clean rucksack. I put it on my back, refuse to give her a kiss, seeing as she specifically asked for one, and risk getting done later by slamming the front door, loudly.

The bus stop is foul. It stinks of piss and alcohol and is full of the smokers. It is an unspoken law that you are not allowed inside the shelter unless you smoke or are in Year 11, which rules out the majority of our village, not that anyone would actually want to go in the bus stop, not out of choice anyway.

Sometimes I get desperate, when it's wet and really cold, and I pretend to smoke just so I can keep dry until the bus comes. Today, I can't be bothered. I'm exhausted and it's only eight-thirty. I say *only* because for the last six blissful weeks I've been in bed at this time, mostly until lunchtime actually, watching Matthew's TV, or at least listening to it booming out of his room, whilst playing on my Nintendo, borrowed from Paul – Paul who also has *Tomb Raider 2* and *3* for the PlayStation. A very good friend to have is Paul. The last six weeks went so quickly. Six weeks sounds like ages when you first hear it, like on 18 July when we broke up. I thought, 'YES!' and that it would stretch out and last forever, but it didn't. There did come a point, about three weeks into the summer, when I thought I might be getting bored but I looked around at all my clothes on the floor, the PlayStation games awaiting my attention and my three rounds of toast on the desk, my magazine that needed reading, and Paul due in half an hour, and realised I didn't have time to think about being bored.

I don't think my mum helped much by giving me lists of things she wanted me to do. Lists! I mean, what am I? Slave labour! Well, that's what I would have said to her if I wasn't scared of getting a mouthful, and I am all for peace and quiet as far as mums go. It's a major drawback having a teacher for a mum 'cos she gets six weeks off too and gets to check up on me and make sure I don't vegetate in front of the TV all day. So I had to plan my mission, to stay in bed for as long as possible, with almost military precision. Mostly, I'd fake getting up by making noises in my room to sound as if I was surfacing, wait until she went to Tesco or to meet her friends, or to keep-fit, then I'd skulk back to bed. It just takes a bit of thought and time really. Still, it's only four days until the weekend when I can have a lie-in, thank God. Just got to make it through the first day back – always the worst. They do this awful extended tutor-time thing, in which you get all this crap paperwork that tries to organise your life. It gets worse once you're on the GCSE slide, according to Matthew, my brother, the world expert and authority on, well, everything now he's at college and no longer incarcerated in Stoneley High, the lucky git.

But no lie-in today. Today I'm going back to school – smelly, stodgy, strict, screaming girls, sports in the cold, school. I sigh and begin the daily argument with the bus driver, who knows from all of last term that I lost my bus pass and that, 'Yes, I do go to Stoneley High, seeing as I'm wearing this foul jumper that says so'. When I ask him if he thinks I just have no taste and am secretly a fashion victim, he mutters at me in bus-driver language, which no pupil can yet interpret, but all kinds of breakthroughs are being made in medical conditions and maybe, one day, the student and the bus driver will be able to understand one another and converse truly. Bus drivers tend to communicate in this language through the apparently compulsory beard, stained yellow by roll-ups – each one a living anti-smoking advertisement. Must be part of the interview:

'Do you smoke roll-ups faster than you can make them?'

'Mumble-mumble-grunt, snort, hack, hack,' would come the unintelligible reply.

'Congratulations, you're now a fully-fledged, grunting, hacking bus driver. Away with you now to scare the wits out of little children. Good man!'

I clamber on to the bus, throw myself into a seat and immediately regret it as my arse makes contact with the steel, slyly-covered with less than a millimetre of foam. I wish I was Matthew and could get lifts to college with Ripper, whose Mini smells exactly like the bus stop, but at least the seats are covered with some form of material that's not going to hospitalise you. Only five miles to go before I have to grunt, kick the floor, swear, slag off teachers, and look totally pissed off. I will just about be able to summon up the energy for all that. Sounds all right actually.

ISLA

Why do they need so many bells? Can they no' tell the time yet? If another grimy boy shoves me he'll wish he never. So, yesterday was ma first day. I was stompin' in ma platforms, no' knowing where I was going, when a lassie came up to me and asked 'Are you Irelar, in 10 HUG?'

'What's 10 hug?' I wasn't sure if this was some code I should have learned, but it wasna in the prospectus they'd sent up to Edinburgh. Apparently, it's the name of ma form, no' some foreign language, although I were tempted to sneer at it like it were. So, 10 HUG = Year 10 + Hughes (Miss Hughes, ma form tutor). I'd cracked it, but couldna see the need to complicate matters any further.

'What's the point in that?' I asked the lassie.

'So you know which form you're in. Look, I'm Georgia, I'll take you. You are Irelar, aren't you?'

I was no' going to hit her, no' on ma first day, but for God's sake, could she no' get ma name right?

'Look, it's Isla. You say it *Ila*, you ken?'

'No . . . I'm Georgia, not Ken. Ken's a boy's name. Are you trying to say I look like a boy?'

By now she was wailing like a banshee, which incidentally wasna a good look for her there, in the hallway with everyone looking an' nudging one another, loving the entertainment, a great start to ma first day in the land of grey drab-looking people.

'No. Look. I were saying, do you *ken*. You know, do-you-*understand*? As in how to say ma name?'

I was really trying then.

'Whatever.' And she stomped off, her perfectly manicured hand held up in protest. So I still didn't know where 10 HUG was, or who Georgia was, an' she couldna say ma name, an' I think I insulted her, the loon! Eventually, I found 10 HUG an' sat well away from banshee-girl, who I now really wanted to call Ken just to annoy her. Georgia – I mean, what kind of a name is that? I thought mine were weird but at least it's from this country. Ever the patriots ma parents.

The lad in front of me handed me about ten different forms an' timetables, an' year planners, an' day books, an' option lists. I'm in Year 10 now. If I were at home I'd be in S3, Secondary Three. I'm doing

GCSEs now. If I were still safely in Scotland I'd be doing ma Standard Grade. I can get anything from A* to E now. If I were still at home I'd get a simple Foundation, General or Credit, then on to ma Highers, none of this A levels or GNVQ lark. I was confused. The lad saw this an' explained: Option A was ma drama; Option B, ma history; Option C ma music; an' Option D ma French.

His name is Luke. He's a wee bit skinny an' has freckles spilt all over his nose but his hair is a lovely glossy black colour, the kind a girl would die for, an' he has eyelashes to match. Typical that a lad should get them. Mine are so pale I have to put at least three coats of mascara on before I can even see them!

Anyway, it doesna matter what his lashes are like as I'm no' going to make friends here, after a day in that place I'm away home on the next train, no stopping me. Bloody GCSEs an' A*s.

LUKE

'*Bonsoir Monsieur. Ça va? Bien? Ce soir, le menu pour dîner est les frites avec—*'

I had to put a stop to this.

'Mum. You are so immature. What if I'd brought someone back with me?'

I hate it when she opens the door wearing her 'French wines and regions' apron and talks in French. She can't even cook. Well, she can really – it's just she's so over the top sometimes, in a mum sort of way. I wonder if it's something that happens to you once you have kids – you suddenly lose all sense of embarrassment? At least I'll never suffer in that way. I am never going to have kids and make them have to choose who to live with when the inevitable happens and divorce comes along. Over half my tutor group's parents are divorced or about to be. Makes you wonder why people bother these days. I'm just going to live with someone – that's presuming someone wants to live with me and all that stuff. I don't have time for all this now – I have to deal with my mum.

'Luke. *Mon petit fils. Viens ici!* What do you mean brought someone back? Who?'

She tries to seem calm but now I am on to a winner. She is curious. Admittedly it doesn't take much to get my mum curious, she seems to have a radar for it – news or gossip, that is. The French talk is gone and she knows something has happened. I am not going to have a conversation about this. I look around the room, suddenly fascinated by the onion, garlic and tomatoes on the chopping board and the stack of French exercise books already on the table after only one day back at school. Matthew bounces in and surveys the scene. Matthew no longer walks. He bounces now that he's in the sixth form. Clearly you have to learn a new walk before they let you into college. In fact, he has grown too tall and gangly for walking. He bounces past me, 'accidentally' shoving me into the door frame, grabs a handful of sliced tomatoes, shoves them into his mouth followed by a can of Coke torn from the fridge and consumed in one tomato-crammed mouthful. He ends his performance with a loud echoing belch. I snigger. Mum laughs. Something is not quite right here but I don't know what.

'You're disgusting,' I inform him, in case he were in any doubt.

'Oh, yeah, and this coming from the windiest region in this house. I hear you every morning, letting rip and—' he instantly retorted. Luckily, Mum interrupted him.

'OK, so now you two have complimented each other on your bodily functions can you please choose: ham or bacon on your pizza?'

'Bacon.' I am quick.

'Ham.' Matthew is too slow.

What matters here is that, 'they might look the same, but they don't taste the same,' as Chris Moyles on Radio One often points out. I give Matthew a victory smile as I run upstairs and beat him to the bathroom. I don't actually want the toilet or a shower yet but I just like to know that should the need arise I can use either, whereas Matthew, poor fool, can use neither until I say so. Almost embarrassingly childish, I know, but I learned from the master and to play one of his own tricks on him is very satisfying now he's all grown up.

It is then, leaning uncomfortably on the chipped window ledge, looking at the grey, dull sky, that I remember the new girl – Isla, Scottish and a bit stroppy. I don't know why I think of her now, in our bathroom. I mean she isn't grey or dull like this sky and . . . oh God! The door is ready to give in to Matthew and part company from its hinges.

'Shut UP!' I advise before he breaks the door down. Right. I think I'll go and check that Lara Croft is still OK. Nothing to do with the fact that Matthew is threatening to cut off various parts of my body and offer them to stray dogs as a delicacy. I decide to let him in, purely so I can play on the computer. No fear.

ISLA

Saturday morning. I stretched ma hands above ma head an' hit the ceiling, almost breaking ma third finger. How was this possible? An unexpected growth spurt overnight? Recognition was slow an' a wee bit painful. I looked around the attic room, trying to focus on the apparently drunken walls sloping over me. So, the leisurely Saturday mornings I was used to were no longer possible. I shuffled up the bed an' sat up, banging ma head hard on the sliding wall behind me. I swore under ma breath as I reached up an' opened ma roof window, which immediately let in a smoggy, smoky smell. I sighed dramatically, slammed the window shut an' sat back down on ma bed, ma head now throbbing. Throbbing o'course is an exaggeration but by now I was in a mood. In order to allow ma mood to develop an' generally ruin the best day of the week was no' difficult an' was made so much easier by Hannah shuffling her way back into the room. 'Back into the room' because, oh joy and rapture, at the mature age of fourteen, I share ma hovel of a room with ma nine-year-old sister, who is a sci-fi geek full time and a computer nerd part time. She has long blonde hair which is totally wasted and left to fend for itself, an' she has a big mouth which reports all ma daily an' probably nightly movements to *them*.

'Are y'awake then?'

A question I choose no' to answer, letting out instead a contemptuous snort combined with a roll of the mascara-smudged eyes.

'What shall we do? Isla? Isla . . . what shall we do now?'

She was sat no' on her own bed, but on the end of mine. How this invasion occurred I'm no' sure, an' the fact that she used the word 'we' had me scared. I ignored her, hoping she'd go away, an' checked the red neon figures on ma radio alarm clock. 8:40 a.m., twenty to nine. So much for ma lie in. I turned around, she was still there an' staring, waiting, sat in her nightie, clutching her Gameboy. It was a real nightie, with cats on, bought specifically to wear to bed. Had she no shame? I was in a huge T-shirt and boxer shorts affair, no' a cat or a puppy dog in sight. Clearly, Hannah needed advice in the fashion department an' if I could have been bothered I would have been the woman to give it. However, I am aware that at nine, fashion is not really a concept you understand as your mum still chooses what you wear an' there is not enough time for Barbie an' Sindy's wardrobe let alone Hannah's own clothes. As it was she was getting on ma nerves already with her big cow eyes staring up at me as if she were expecting me to pull a rabbit out of a hat or something.

'Look, Hannah, *we* are doing nothing. I'm after some breakfast, an' then I'm away into town an' you are definitely no' coming.'

Downstairs, there was no breakfast, no *them*, and a note.

Isla and Hannah,
We've had to go into the Post Office. Ellie is ill.
There's a key in the jar on the windowsill. Isla, do not leave Hannah on her own please. There's left-overs in the fridge for lunch. Put them in the microwave on number 5.
We'll be back at about ten to seven.
Lots of love
Mum and Dad
xx

No, no, no! It was so unfair. I didn't even know who Ellie was. Saturday! I should have been watching *Live and Kicking*, eating crunchy peanut butter and black-currant jam on toast – a foul concoction to anyone except ma friend Lucy and me – then on to wash ma hair, put on make-up, pick out ma clothes, meet the girls at the bus stop and into town. None of this should ever have to involve Hannah, leftovers, microwaves or a key. I didn't want sci-fi geek attached to ma arse all day.

I like knowing they are at home while I'm out. It's like I've been gone ages when I come in an' I show them what I got in the sale in Top Shop and tell Hannah about the fire eaters and the twenties singers on the Royal Mile. It's like I'm famous for a little while an' we get on then. She listens an' I have something interesting to say. I don't mind her so much in small doses, but forced upon me without prior warning is no' fair – even if she is ma sister, I still need ma space.

I like to burst noisily into the house, bags in ma hands, them no' knowing what time to expect me, an' if it's been snowing or raining ma mum will offer me hot chocolate an' I'll get the chance to wind Hannah up an' really see how gullible she is an' what she'll believe. Then she'll bug me until I cave in under the power of the blue eyes that trust so much I canny continue, but it's good crack all the while, an' harmless, as she knows ma game really. She'll stare piercingly until she's got all the details of the day an' the girls an' the events out of me, listening attentively to ma tales, making mental notes, watching an' waiting to trip me up, until I giggle and give maself away, then she'll giggle too an' it's like we're in it together.

I found maself rereading the note, sighing heavily. I wanted to go home, to Scotland.

Hannah slumped down opposite me, still staring an' looking.

'I read the note. They're away to work for the day. What shall we do, Isla?'

I sighed an' put ma throbbing head on the cold, hard table.

LUKE

Sunday must be the longest day of the week but as no one else has yet discovered it, it remains a secret. One day, I will discover the theory behind it and explain to people why shops will only open at ten and close at four, why TV is a 'no go area', devoid of the colour and promise it offers me Monday to Saturday. I shall reveal, much like David Copperfield, the truth behind the myth that you must eat a huge roast dinner, feel full and probably sick. I will astound the nation with my explanation of the common myth that the youngest member of the household must, on this fateful day, walk the dog, even when it is clearly not their turn. I shall solve the mystery shrouding why – when you've had all week and a full day on Saturday – why at 7:30 p.m. on Sunday night, if you haven't already lost all of your senses, why you choose then to attempt four different kinds of homework, including a lame mini-PSHE project.

PSHE! Personal, Social and Health Education.

What makes it worse is that we're doing drugs. Not actually taking them, but learning about them from Miss Hughes and a policeman who doesn't like us. He shakes his head and looks at us as if to say, 'I know what you're like,' and tells us about Leah Betts and Ecstasy. Like we don't know, like we don't know all that and more – more than he ever will. He doesn't have to go down the all-weather football pitch, Stoneley's unofficial youth club, getting hassle and being teased when you try and tell them you're not there to score but actually to try and play five-a-side. It's much harder *not* to buy. I don't. It's not just that it's drugs and illegal, 'cos I do other stuff that's illegal. Well, I have a drink every now and then, but it's well expensive and it makes you hungry, and basically you sound like an idiot laughing at, well, nothing really. And then there's the paranoia. You think everyone's staring at you, or laughing at you, it's too weird. So I say no or pretend I can't hear them. It's just not me. I don't want to become a heavy-lidded, munchie-gripped spliff-head, and that's just the girls.

So, Miss Hughes has set us this project. We have to find four types of drugs in our house, bring them in and explain to 10 HUG what they are. This is going to be so embarrassing. There is no way I'm going to stand up in front of Jason Hassel and Danny Drummond and talk about drugs. They wouldn't need to look in their houses, they could just empty their pockets and fill the table with their little speed-filled rectangular wraps made out of magazines, and their lumps of hash wrapped up in their mum's cling-film. I hate them. They'll just take the piss out of everything Miss Hughes says, they think they know so much, just 'cos they're friends with some sixth form-ers and they think they know all there is to know. The Gaggle don't help.

'The Gaggle' are the sad blonde posse who follow Jason and Danny around as if they're on leads. To be in the Gaggle you have to be blonde, natural or bot-tle, wear tight, pink hoodies, and have a lot of mascara caked over your eyelashes. And, of course, you have to smoke and reek of cheap perfume to cover the stale ashtray odour that lingers around you. The Gaggle are the support act for Jason and Danny. Any time either of them cracks one of their pathetic jokes, usu-ally involving farting, the Gaggle break into almost rapturous peals of hysterical laughter, whilst the rest of us groan. The Gaggle tend to get pissed or stoned every lunchtime with whatever Jason and Danny sup-ply into their eager beaks that day. They make it their mission to turn up late to every registration, looking as if they have smudged red lipstick around their tiny eyes which are so bloodshot they don't even try to hide it. You can imagine how funny they find PSHE lessons on drugs. As I said to Isla, they could run the session if only they could stand upright long enough.

Miss Hughes . . . We – me and Davey and Paul – reckon this is her first job, she's well young. She's nice, but gets really stroppy when we don't shut up in PSHE. And that time when Andrew James threw Davey's rucksack right out of our window in M13, when Miss Clydean and Mr Hills were watching, she went ballistic, screeching about how it made her look in front of the headmaster.

So, to the kitchen to locate Mum's stash, or the teabags and coffee, at least.

She's there, sat at the table, crying, no, not crying, sort of making whimpering noises, snuffling and gulping. In front of her is a calculator, a pen – not red for once – and lots of envelopes and mail and stamps. Bills. Shit. I stand in the doorway, balancing on one foot, my hands shoved into my jeans pockets. I don't know what to do. I'm rubbish at this stuff. God, where's Matthew?

'Where's Matthew?' comes out of my chewed

mouth 'cos I don't know what else to say.

My mum jumps and screams all at the same time.

'Luke! . . . I didn't, um, see you there. I'm sorry. I'm a bit— Matthew? He's down at The George with his mates. So, hmmm, what are you doing skulking out there?' As all this is being said she's shoving the papers, stamps and figures under the newspaper and wiping her messed-up eyes, smudging them even more. She does not look good. This does not look good.

'Mum, what's all that stuff? Is that why you're crying?' I think this is a good start. Promising. Sensible, almost.

'No, no love. Look, I'm just a bit cross with work. They don't pay me enough and every now and then it gets to me. Silly really. But look, I'm fine, really. I think I'll have a bath. Make us a cup of tea?'

She puts her hand on my hair and sort of strokes it, then kisses the top of my head, for too long really, but I don't jerk away as I don't quite know what to do now. It makes everything a bit difficult when people cry, you can't talk as loud or move as quickly as you would normally – you don't want to frighten them. So I do as she asks and make her a cup of tea, probably her tenth of the day. She drinks loads of it, not your regular PG Tips, but Earl Grey, nice-smelling stuff, like lemons I think. It's foul to drink though. Doesn't taste of anything. Pepsi-Max is much better.

I look at her papers, not to read the letters but to try and see what made her cry. Then, once I discover the crisp, starchy envelope with my dad's slanted, scratchy handwriting on it I'm halfway there. Five minutes later, on my own in the kitchen, with the sound of the taps running upstairs and the absence of sound from Matthew's room, my mum is not the only one crying in our house tonight.

ISLA

Two weeks. That's fourteen days. Ten spent incarcerated at Stoneley. That's too many hours to think about an' to make matters all the worse it's Friday. Normally, Fridays would definitely get ma lips curving, ma toes tapping an' ma tummy flipping over at the prospect of the weekend, but no' here. Here, we have PSB or PCE or something equally as stupid. I don't know why they have to keep replacing their words with initials an' all these abbreviations; it's as if they've no time for full sentences. So, anyway, Friday was PS-thing an' I had to tell 10 HUG about four drugs in ma house. It was so painful. I had to stand in front of the class an' none of them could understand ma accent, except Luke, an' he was in a real state, no help at all, an' I still had to do most of ma talk.

Miss Hughes had asked me if I would like to go next. Now, Miss Hughes is all right but she'd no idea of what I'd like to do, an' going next was no' on ma list. But I kinda felt sorry for her, as if she were new too. The Gaggle were failing to smother their laughter when she looked to see if they could stand. It didna look good, so I reluctantly got up, armed with ma teabags, Anadins an' the like, an' did ma thing. Andrew James, prompted by Jason an' that Danny, asked loads of tricky questions an' said he couldna understand me an' could I repeat that again? When I was on the verge of kneecapping the little fungus, Luke jumped out of his chair an' got right in Andrew's face an' shouted at him, with bits of spit escaping from his mouth. I think it went something like:

'Why don't you go and ask the zoo if they still have your cage? You loser!' Then he slammed out of the room.

Of course the whole class cheered and whooped and, loving all the drama, I elected maself to go and see 'if Luke's all right'. Miss Hughes gave me five minutes, and ordered everyone to, 'Sit back down. At once!' As I ran down the corridor, I could still hear her telling Andrew James that he could not 'go and smash Luke's head into his arse'.

Luke was outside on the steps. He looked really small suddenly. He doesn't normally. Normally, he has to duck under the bars in PE, and get down the test tubes for the Poisoned Dwarf in science, and reach up for the books in the library for banshee-girl 'cos she's so small and wee and cute and canny reach by herself.

'Luke?' I didna know what else to say. I put ma hand on his shoulder an' was shocked to feel it jiggling about a wee bit. He was crying. He mumbled something into his shirt sleeve.

'What? Luke, I canny understand. You've to lift your head. Luke?'

'It's my dad. He wrote to my mum. I hate him.' He quickly wiped his eyes on the cuff of his shirt, which I carefully did *not* notice.

'And that's bad – why?' I had no tact but I still didna know what was going on.

'He left my mum, seven or eight years ago, for— and now he won't pay for me and Matthew anymore, and we're really expensive and eat loads and my mum works really hard but she still needs his stupid money.'

I was stunned. No' because of what he'd told me but because he *had* told me. I wanted to say something reassuring an' suggest a plan which could help him an' ask if he had asked his mum about his dad but it had become cold and dark, as if the sun had gone in. I shivered an' we both raised our heads in search of the warm sun, an' met Mr Bourgoine's face far too close for comfort. He was standing in front of us, his black cape swinging behind him causing a wind, almost certainly an ill one. There was no point arguing. We'd been outside too long. The end of our talk had come in the form of the Deputy Head = Trouble.

LUKE

Following our fifty minutes of after-school detention for what was classed as a 'serious offence' – for which your parents are written to on headed school note-paper and telephoned by the Head of Year who has to speak in a deep quiet voice because it's all so serious – we finally went and got chips and sat in the park, whilst we waited for the bus.

We being me and Isla. She got a detention for leaving the classroom and not returning within the specified amount of time. AWOL in army terms. I got one for calling Andrew James an offensive name, disrupting a lesson and displaying a tendency towards violent behaviour.

We had to formally apologise to Miss Hughes in Miss Clydean's office, and Miss Hughes said she had 'no option available' to her other than to put me on report. Complete overreaction for the Head of Year's benefit, but I suppose she has to look hard and strict and stuff when there's other teachers around. I have a strong suspicion my mum will go loopy and put her head in her hands and say melodramatic things like 'this is the last straw' and tell me in a quiet voice that shakes with danger that I've let her down. I'm going to have to tell her what Andrew James has been saying to Isla and she'll probably tell me something like it would have been more appropriate to inform Andrew that he is displaying 'racist tendencies in his anti-Celtic attitude'. She talks like Miss Hughes sometimes, when she's talking about what she calls 'social issues'. I forget she's probably some other kid's tutor and not just my mum. I won't tell her that I know about my dad and the money and the letter.

Isla thinks we should get Saturday jobs. I need one because I eat so much and grow so quickly, and Isla needs one because she hates Saturdays and babysitting Hannah, her sister. I don't think she hates her sister, it's just that nine-year-olds aren't all that interesting and definitely not at the weekend.

We sit on the swings for quite a bit, waiting for the late bus. I know my mum will have cooked something but somehow chips seems to make waiting easier. It gives me something to do with my hands and if I run out of things to say I can just stuff my face. It isn't a problem though. We don't talk about my dad any-more as I feel stupid and Isla isn't particularly nosey. Instead, we invent plots of revenge against Andrew James, and try to work out how old Miss Hughes is and whether she is secretly going out with Mr Owens the PE teacher.

'D'ya reckon they are then, you know together, a couple like? He's really good looking though, muscly an' fit, an', well, she's . . . not.'

I eat my chips rather than risk a comment as I am not sure where she's going with this.

'Luke, do you fancy her?'

I can't believe she can just ask me things like that. I mean, of course I don't fancy her, she's my teacher for God's sake. But, sometimes, when I'm looking at her I forget and then— but no, definitely not, no way.

'No way, she's a teacher, no one fancies the teachers at our school, unless . . . unless you have recently arrived from a foreign place where it is the national custom and pastime to fall in love with, hmmm . . . sports teachers, for example. Could that be the source of this whole conversation, Isla? Being from a foreign place yourself, I couldn't help but notice the coincidence there?' I risk teasing her back.

She stops swinging immediately and lands her feet

on the floor to steady herself before fixing me with a glare to set off her declarations of denial. Oh shit! I've pushed it too far. You just never bloody know with girls, do you?

'Luke! You are talking complete arse. O'course I don't. If I were to fancy someone it wouldna be anyone who were in line for his pension this year.' She looks at me thoughtfully and I catch a glimmer of something in her brown eyes and wonder if it belongs to Andrew James.

I decide not to push her any further, mostly because I don't really know how to play this game of teasing and questioning. No doubt I will ask the wrong questions, safer to stick to the simple things, like swinging. Less shouting involved in that.

We carry on swaying back and forth, almost swinging, casually, not like kids who really try to go high, and she tells me about Scotland and why they left. It was to do with her Gran and her Post Office and shop. She can't run them anymore, her Gran, because she's ill. Isla thinks cancer but no one will tell her and her sister. Why do they think we're too young or that we won't understand? It's worse, the not knowing, not being told and having to sneak about and listen to telephone conversations and trying to guess, because the unknown is scarier. What's in your head is always scarier than the truth because your imagination has to go into overdrive and what you piece together is always a million miles away from what's actually happening. If they would just tell us straight off in the first place, we wouldn't have to spend all the time worrying about our parents. If only they'd think first.

Eventually, Isla's bus comes and she goes. I don't tell her that I don't actually need a bus, and walk home, kicking one stone. I made it all the way.

ISLA

The noise coming from the kitchen wasn't a clanking, chopping, cupboards and fridge doors opening, dinner is on the way type of noise. It was more of a musical noise, ma mum's voice rising up an' down, like a scale, interrupted by ma dad's deep, rumbling one, like a bass drum, jumping to a different beat. They sounded like two members of an orchestra fighting against one another – the battle between the boom of the drums versus the screeching of the violins. It didn't sound very harmonious or hopeful. I shut the front door behind me an' dumped ma bag in the cupboard under the stairs, shoving the door shut without looking where ma bag ended up. I'd regret that in the morning as I hadna done up the zip.

Hannah was sat at the top of the stairs, her chin on her knees, her hair falling messily out of its French plait. She looked up, a mixture of anticipation and relief. More pressure! I climbed up to her and nudged her over. We squashed up together an' I felt her relax against me. She looked really worried, her little forehead all lines and creases.

'What's the deal, eh?' I thought she may know, being highly advanced in the skills of spying.

'Money . . . I think. There's been mention of a flat an' Tennants beer an'—'

I stopped her there. Now, obviously the money part made sense but the rest of her information was suspect an' probably originated from the dark depths of her overactive, computer-enhanced imagination.

'What flat?' I chose to tackle the beer issue, if there was one, later.

'The one above Gran's shop.'

Oh God, no. No!

'What about it?' I tried cautiously, no' really wanting to hear James Bond's answer.

'I think . . . I think—' She put her head further down and wouldna look at me.

'Hannah.' I borrowed ma mum's sternest voice.

'I think we might be going to live there?' She looked out from under her heavy fringe an' straggly hair to measure ma anger.

'An' the beer?' I asked through gritted teeth but the answer came from the violin voice in the kitchen.

'Tha's right, go on then, open another can 'cos that'll sort it out, no?'

An' then the boom.

'Och, for God's sake, Beth, this is the first! Look, we've no choice. We canny live here an' run the shop. There's empty flat space above it, an' we can rent out here an' the lassies can walk to school from the Post Office. It makes sense, eh?'

That explained it was *tenants* an' not Tennants an' cleared Hannah of the charges of an overactive imagination, for now. Well, it all seemed fairly conclusive then – once again, another decision had been made for us by them, without our consent. Did they never think to talk to us, to ask us how we felt about something like moving from our home again!

I knew what ma dad would say if I tried to explain how I felt, if I said I was fourteen an' needed to make ma own choices. He would rant about bills, an' the mortgage, an' his job, an' how he works fierce hard for us, an' all I do is complain, an' leave the TV on, an' all the upstairs lights, an' haven't I any consideration for anyone else in this house other than maself? Then ma mum would join forces with him. They tend to stick together in the face of battle, even if they've just been doing a good impression of thunder an' lightning rowing in the kitchen. She would tell me that when I am older I will understand, an' that they were in a difficult position, an' when I had kids I would have tough choices to make too! As if! I am not having kids or getting married or having rows with someone over bills and stuff. I am going to live in New York or Paris in an apartment an' do what I want, an' leave all the lights and the TV on if I want, an' have peanut butter and chocolate spread sandwiches at three in the morning an' not get told off.

Once I calmed down I tried to work out how the four of us would live in the wee doll's house flat over Gran's Post Office. That's when Hannah reminded me of her presence an' started crying. No, not again. Twice in two weeks – first Luke and now her. I put ma arms around her and felt very old an' no' very fourteen.

'Come on now, Hannah. Come on now, hen, it'll be all right. It'll be fine, hen.'

Somehow, I don't think she believed me.

LUKE

Dave's Deli. I want a job in the arcade but I don't think Isla will be too keen. We only have one day, Saturday, to find ourselves jobs, together. We have decided safety in numbers is the best policy.

So, the chippie is out – we'd get spotty and greasy-haired and obese. So are pubs because we're too young. Well, I definitely am, but I reckon Isla could pass for seventeen, maybe eighteen, when she wears all that make-up stuff and does her 'older hairstyle'. No restaurants will take us, we're too inexperienced. Because we can't sell cigarettes, got to be sixteen, newsagents are out. That leaves Dave's Deli. Right up in the Plaza shopping arcade, at the very end, lurking underneath a green and white stripy awning and sign, and with lots of fruit piled on fake green moss.

Inside, it is undeniably bright. Hideous artificial white flickering strips of neon glare out over the whole shop. It sells tea and coffee and cake and the most healthy vegetarian, herbal-type food you can think of. No Pepsi-Max but carrot and lemongrass juice, pulped wheatgrass, liquorice sticks and rows of vitamins for the suckers who buy them. My mum gives me a vitamin C tablet every morning but it's OK because it tastes like a sweet. I don't think it actually does anything. It's all in the mind. I took five once to see what would happen, to see if I would develop skin with a tinge of orange or become really well and full of energy. Nothing changed, I stayed exactly the same. They're a con, vitamins, they've got to be. That means all the other herbal remedies and vitamin supplements are probably a rip-off too! Maybe I should do an exposé, work undercover and go to the BBC with my findings. Maybe not . . . maybe I should stick to finding a job. Sometimes I lose it a bit and my mind runs away with ideas like it used to when I was little – make-believe, let's-pretend stuff. Thank God these thoughts stay in my head and don't come out of my mouth. What would Isla think of me then?

It's hard being stuck in the middle sometimes. At fourteen you are sort of nowhere really. Too old to behave like a kid but too young to really do anything. That's why I need a job, a bit of independence and some money to go out with, without having to rely on my mum to pick us up in her bloody Volvo.

At the back of the shop, which is narrow and long, is a cake counter – baked daily on these premises – and four tables, white with green chairs, so people can sit and have a coffee and cake, which costs more than if you have exactly the same but choose to eat it in your own home and not sat on a green garden chair in here – total rip-off.

Isla and I are waiting for the manager, Dave. We wonder if he'll be green or white. Isla goes with green, I think white is favourite. He is neither. He is a ruddy colour, as if someone has taken a brillo pad to his face. He is wearing stonewashed jeans, white socks and black slip-on golfing shoes with tassles. He is also parading a Welsh rugby shirt and a dirty apron, white in its previous life but not now it has the misfortune to be tied tightly round his overspill of a gut. He has stubble and is wearing quite a lot of gold jewellery for just one person.

'So yous two are here for the job then, are you? Right then, what experience have you had then?'

He says all this to Isla, ignoring me. He has a deep rolling voice, a strong Welsh accent and even stronger breath. Isla moves back a little, opens her mouth and lies. Massively.

'We've both worked in a teashop an' Luke's mum is

a tea expert, an' I'm a vegetarian, an' we both know how to work a till an' we're honest an'—'

I'm impressed. So is Dave.

'So, your mam's an expert is she? Do you know how to cook? Can you bake?'

To me now. I look at Isla, she nods and I follow her lead.

'Yeah. I do home economics at school and I'm always making pizzas at home.'

Lie. Lie. Lie.

'Right, well. It just so 'appens I am needing two Saturday kids aren't I? So, yous two are lucky now, aren't you? Right, see you next Saturday then. Seven-thirty sharp. Help to set up. Mind you tie that pretty hair back now.' Dave moves in closer to Isla and points to her hair which swooshes around quite a bit, then he strides back into the kitchen.

We are ecstatic. We try not to run outside, back into the sun. It isn't until later, on the swings in the park, with chips, that we try to work out how much we will earn.

'Well, if we're starting at seven-thirty and work till about six, that's ten, ten and a half hours, take off one for lunch, nine and a half, that must be loads of money, no?'

Isla is smiling, swinging, pleased, so I don't remind her that it's still dark at six-thirty when we'll have to get up and dress in time to get into town. Maybe Mum'll give us a lift. I wish I were old enough to drive us. It's so embarrassing being picked up and dropped off and everyone watching you knowingly as you get out of your mum's car. It always makes me angry and wonder how they got there. It's as if some people at school are too sussed to reveal the fact that they have a parent, keeping them safely within the confines of their home.

Like at school discos, you have to get there really early or really late if you don't want to face the line-up of people sat on the wall smoking and staring and swigging casually from their designer bottles of beer, screwing up their eyes to assess your car and what you're wearing and whether or not you have had the stupidity to let a parent drop you off. Inevitably the parent pursues you loudly with shouts of times and curfews as you charge off into the night, disowning them with a hissed 'Goodbye', which when translated clearly means 'please pull away from the kerb as quickly as you can, without waving and do not return at ten o'clock to collect me as I will die a social death'. You hope your tone of voice and facial expression manages to convey all this clearly enough for the poor things, who once they reached the age of thirty forgot anything that ever happened to them between the ages of eleven and nineteen. Parents really shouldn't be allowed out unless they are trained.

If I ever have kids I will not be an annoying parent. I am going to be one of those liberal parents who let their kids call them by their first names rather than Mummy and Daddy! I will be thoughtful enough to give them money for a taxi so they don't get embarrassed, and I will let them buy their own clothes and stay out late if they want and generally let them decide what they want to do, within reason of course.

ISLA

Even after the fifth Saturday morning, six-thirty still seemed too early to leave the feather pillows, but having ma own money was kinda good, an' the feeling tired an' brave at the end of a long day an' coming in looking like you've seen some sights during the day. I loved telling tales of snobby customers, and when Madonna came in. She walked past, anyway, an' looked like she was definitely thinking about coming in.

I dressed quickly, no' caring what I looked like as no one interesting came into Dave's Belly – they canny make it past the green and white. Luke had renamed Dave's Deli the week before. He had a bad day there. The previous four had no' been too hectic, actually, but last Saturday was really busy. As I left the house to catch the bus I took the rain as a bad sign. Luke was already there when I got to the bus stop. I smiled at him an' he smiled back, peeping out from under his hood of hair darkened by droplets of rain. It would be OK.

By lunch break things were no' OK. By *lunch break* I mean the half an hour, which we're no' allowed to spend together in case it gets too busy. So lunch break is boring an' a wee bit lonely, wandering around town, looking aimlessly in the shops, secretly shoving a sandwich into your mouth that you'd lifted from work. Made by your own fair hands at nine that morning, it somehow doesna taste too wonderful. We've started making each other's lunch an' it has to be a surprise an' inventive. You're no' allowed to use a filling more than the once, an' the more weird and wonderful the better. I'm in the lead with crunchy peanut butter and chocolate spread.

I came back from ma lunch break, lingered in the disgustin' staff toilet for as long as legally possible, fiddlin' with ma hair until I realised Luke couldna go for his lunch until I took over from him. I ran down the stairs no' touching the greasy, damp walls, an' fought ma way through the queue of daft people hovering by the cake counter. What's the point in that? Why no' go somewhere else to eat, somewhere nice maybe? Luke looked really miserable. I was late an' felt guilty.

'Sorry! Uh, oh . . . what's the deal, eh? Dave been giving you a hard time, no?'

I nudged him as he didna answer me.

'Hmm. Look. I'll see you after my break.' He moved softly past me, his long arms reaching behind his back to untie the double knot in his grimy apron, but stopped, dropping his arms when he saw Dave marching over to the counter we were both stood behind.

'Great, here we go,' Luke muttered with his head down.

'So. Where do you think you are going then, lovely boy? Hmm? I don't think you deserve a break now do you?'

'Dave, it's quarter to two and I'm starving. You've got Karen on the till, and Isla is back. What's the problem?' The last bit of the question sounded a wee bit dangerous through Luke's voice an' I think even Dave caught it.

'So. You don't know what the problem is? It's *you*. You haven't cleaned the drips tray of the Espresso machine or emptied the bins. You are lazzyyyyy. Now get that apron back on and serve these people here . . . stupid bugger!'

Luke's eyes flashed as he jerked up his head. Stupid? I couldna believe the cheek of him. I looked up an' down the queue of middle-aged beige people who only cared about how much froth they got on their cappuccinos, and were clearly not listening to the way Dave was treating Luke. They had no idea that Luke's dad wouldn't pay for him an' so he had no alternative but to slave and skivvy here, making sure their milk was warm enough for their precious coffees an' their chocolate roulades creamy enough for their delicate taste buds. I exploded.

'How dare you? Who d'ya think y'are, eh? You are nothing but a big, an' I mean *big*, bully. Luke works fierce hard here an' for two pounds an hour! An' now, now you won't give him a lunch break? Well, that's it, you can find yourself two more slaves. Dave's Belly can stick its crappy jobs!'

I grabbed Luke's hand, charged down to Karen's till, took a twenty out, my hand shaking, an' strode out of the shop, ma head held high. When we got outside an' round the corner of Blackjack Street we both cracked up.

'Oh my God, Isla. You are mad. I can't believe you did that. It was brilliant! No one has stuck up for me before, well, not like that. Thanks.' An' then he kissed me, Luke, on ma cheek an' it sort of grew, fluttering down to ma lips. Are we going out together now? I know I'm racing on an' that, but Luke . . . kissed . . . me!

LUKE

We've walked out. Well, Isla walked out and took me with her. She also took twenty pounds out of the till. She learned how to cash up last week, so she knew how to open it. Dave owed us at least twenty pounds, probably more for unpaid overtime. I haven't got a job now but it was worth it to see Dave's face and watch his rat's eyes widen and his huge mouth fall open when Isla yelled at him. She said everything so fast that I wish we'd had a tape. I hope Dave understood it all, her accent gets incredibly strong when she's stroppy.

It's getting dark and we still haven't quite made it home. Isla has to get the 54 bus to West Stoneley and I have to get the 53, unless I get off at the third stop and walk from hers. Anyway, we don't want to go home yet as there'll be questions for me, and Hannah waiting for Isla, ready to report apparently. She sounds worse than Matthew. So to the bat cave, or the bus stop as it's more commonly known. We've got twenty pounds but we decide not to break into it as I have enough fare for us. Isla folds the twenty into her Kangol wallet until we decide what to do with it. We are sat next to each other upstairs even though there's loads of spare seats on the bus downstairs. No one sits downstairs, unless they're old. I suppose it's easier than following the steel rail as it spirals its way up unsteady stairs. I always run up, normally while the bus is pulling off. I don't know why, I just do. I run up the stairs at home, too, even if I'm not in a hurry. It annoys my mum.

You can tell something has happened. We are sat, still and silent, but sort of smiling. I quickly look at Isla. I kissed her. I didn't know I was going to. She's got little rumpled lines in between the freckles on her forehead. Right on her cheek and then I carried it on to her lips. She really stuck up for me. She's so brave, to do that, to shout at Dave. I mean, I want to smack his face in, to land my fist into his squidgy, fleshy cheek and see him reel back into the cake counter with cream mashed into his hair but I know it's not going to happen. Isla makes stuff happen. Isla made me kiss her.

I've kissed before, obviously, proper kissing down the all-weather football pitch. I even got Davey to ask both Lisa Peaker and Jackie Drummond, Danny's younger sister, both times so I knew there would be no chancing, I wouldn't want to make an arse of myself.

But this wasn't prepared and that's scary, especially as it was all me and none of her. At least if you've asked them, it's both your faults if it goes wrong and you know for definite they are there, willing, and are going to kiss you and you hope it'll be all right and maybe lead to . . . Anyway, I don't know if Isla is crumpling up her face because I've kissed her and ruined everything, or not?

She has just seen me staring. I stop. We go back to looking at different things. She stands to get off at her stop and I stand too but I'm not sure.

'You getting off here? It's no' far to walk then?'

She speaks. I breathe out. So it's OK then. I follow her down the steps and repeat her thanks to the bus driver, who grunts. No idea what that's supposed to mean. I decide to leave the translation for another time and jump off, wondering whether it's still OK to walk her home, not walk her home as in a couple-type activity but to walk along with her until we get to her home and then sort of carry on to mine.

'Luke? You've no' said anything for ages? You OK?

Gonna walk me to ma house?'

'Yeah, sure.' I really want to say more to show I'm not being silent and awkward but suddenly I can't think of anything to say. How is it that, normally, we fight for space, pushing in front of one another, with words to say and sibling stories to appal one another, and now I can't think of anything to say other than:

'Look Isla, I hope, I mean, kissing you, well, are you in a mood now?' Apparently, this is what I choose to say. I don't really want to know if she's in a mood. That's the last thing I want to know. I can't imagine wanting to know anything less. I only want to know if everything is all right. I'm not stupid, I do not want to delve into the unknown territory of female mood swings without some form of artillery or protection.

'Luke, what are you talking about? It were only a wee kiss, no' a full blown snog. No problem OK?'

I can't believe she said snog, we never talk like that, we never use words like that because we have never needed to. So what does this mean? Is it all completely back to normal and forgotten? I mean, I kissed her. Doesn't she care? Isn't she mad? Maybe it was crap, maybe I was.

'So I'll see you on Monday then?'

'What?' Then I see she's leaning against the post

box outside her house, well, her flat. That happened quickly. I nod to show that I've understood and am not a total idiot although I've still lost the power of sensible speech and all my conversational skills. I walk home, ignoring the kicking potential that lies in many stones.

ISLA

I'm shocked and cross with about three different people an' for entirely different reasons. When I got in I knew there wouldna be any pleased faces once I broke ma news of 'The Great Storming Out' an' the whole no' having a job anymore thing, but to see ma mum an' dad and Hannah all sat there on the sofa we'd shoved into the tiny lounge, in silence – no music, no telly – it was surreal an' made ma tummy flip over.

'What?' I decided attack was definitely the best form of defence.

'Isla. Sit down, we need to talk.' Coming from ma dad, now this did no' look too hot, he hated talking at the best of times.

'Hannah, go to your room, now, please.' This from ma mum wasn't a request but more of a demand. I inwardly gulped and outwardly scrunched up ma face as Hannah reluctantly left the room, making sure she left the door ajar. I sat down, messily, scattering my things around me, a moat of protection from the advancing attack. There didn't seem much point in arguing or slamming off to ma room as Hannah was in there an' the room can only take two people, that's if you're both lying down on your beds, an' I was too jumpy to lie anywhere. Ma head was running with a variety of things I might have done. Only one really stood out, though, if I were being truthful.

'Dave rang us at the shop, in the middle of the Saturday afternoon rush, the busiest time o' the day. In the middle of all this he informs me that he's considering ringing the police. The police, Isla! Because, you have stolen thirty pounds from him. Now [laughing] obviously I tell him he's made a mistake there, as ma daughter would never steal, but then a Karen lass comes on the phone an' tells me it's true. So then I ask to speak with ma daughter, but she's no' there, she's walked off. Now this was five hours ago. So for the last five hours we've been wondering where the hell in the middle of Maidstone our daughter could be.'

His voice had done the climbing thing where, when he's mad, it gets louder an' deeper an' more out of control, until he's on the brink of swearing at me, an' ma mum has to take over with her fake I-am-sooooocalm voice, which gets higher an' shriller as the calmness she ordered fails to turn up.

I could feel the bubble of denial trapped in ma lungs. I pulled ma rucksack into me, hugging it, poised, ready an' armed, the money lurking guiltily in ma wallet at the bottom of ma bag.

'I didn't steal thirty pounds. Dave owed me an' Luke, an' it was only twenty I took. He owes us loads more but I didn't take that.'

It sounded lame even to me. I know I shouldn't have helped maself but there was no way I was going to ask for it an' I knew Dave would never give it. Ma mum geared up as ma dad moved over to let her step in for her turn, whilst he supported her by shaking his head over an' over.

'You shouldna have helped yourself, it's no' your till. Imagine how your dad an' I would feel if Ellie had o' done that, eh? Now look, Isla, I managed to convince Dave no' to phone the police.'

I sighed and let the trapped bubble escape. I was kinda glad ma mum had intervened, sometimes you really do just need a mum to sort it all out.

'All you have to do is write a letter of apology.'

I couldna believe she slipped this in at the end. I almost missed it, it was so quick. They both sat back as I jumped up in ma seat where I had been slumped, marooned by ma lack of ground to stand on. But this, a letter?

'No way. No way. I've done nothing wrong, he owed it to us. I canny believe you're taking his side.' I could hear ma voice going whiny an' high.

'Theft, Isla. A police record. Is that what you're wanting at fourteen?'

I had to admit that this was quite a good point, well made an' annoying in its simplicity. So I had to do it, there didn't seem to be a way out, nowhere to stomp to, unless . . .

'I'm going out.'

'Where? It's dark. It's too late, Isla. Why don't you just get it over with and write the letter?'

Seeing as this didn't appeal I continued with ma theory – better out than in.

'I'm away to Luke's. It's only three roads away and you can ring me there if there's any more correspondence you'd like me to do.'

I knew I was being a pain an' difficult an' displaying the classic symptoms of a turbulent teenager but I didn't want to write to Dave an' I definitely didn't want to say sorry or agree with ma parents about ma narrow escape. So Luke's seemed a better option. I'd

been there before an' his mum seemed more reason-
able than mine. I knew Luke would understand why I
couldna write this letter even though I knew I would
have to do it, but just not right then.

LUKE

Matthew is setting up his Internet access and e-mail address in his room, muttering about modems and set-up installations, fiddling with cables and swearing at figures that fill the computer screen. He has compiled a new system from Ripper's old one which he thinks is outdated but Matthew keeps saying it's a total waste to kill off this classic machine and with a bit of time and effort it'll be up and running. This was, of course, four days ago and he's been devoting all his precious time to gaining a 'connection' so he can 'communicate' with people 'out there' because, as he told my mum, the phone is 'like, totally outdated now'.

He has just told me for the third time, as I tried to sneak past his room, that he's 'nearly there now'. Poor, disillusioned fool, if he is ever going to get there I hope it is soon, it's almost painful to see him with his head tucked under his desk, wriggling about with leads and regularly banging his head. Under desks is not where he should be. As I try to creep by to go downstairs and investigate the fridge he pokes his head out of the debris and asks me to help. I haven't been invited into his room for many years and have never been asked for my help before. I decide to brave the toxic fumes and mouldy plates that lurk beneath jumpers and in his desk drawers, and enter the room. Why he can't tuck them neatly under the bed is a mystery.

'What do you want me to do?'

'Hold that. No, that! Hold it away from the desk so I can pass you up the modem wire, then pull it through the thingy.'

Apparently all the technical terms have gone to Computer Genius's head and he assumes I am familiar with the 'thingy'. I improvise and pull a cord up from the back of the desk and wait, not really appreciating the shouting, especially as I am clearly invaluable in this operation.

'Right, so put it in the left socket, the one without the phone picture next to it. Make sure it goes in the left one. Gently for God's sake, Luke, that cost fifteen quid!'

I put the lead in, hope and quickly move away.

'Ow! Watch my leg you idiot!' Matthew jumps as I

tread on his long legs which are lying across the floor, and manages to add to his injury by catching his elbow on the side of the desk leg. Swearing loudly he leaps up. I move further away, for safety's sake; the room isn't that big. But he sits down at the desk and throws his hands really quickly over the keyboard, and types in loads of letters and slashes and symbols, which make no sense to me. And I'm not convinced he understands them, until I hear the computer making alien noises, like someone gargling with mouthwash down the phone. This, according to Matthew's reaction, is a good thing.

'Yes! Excellent, I'm in. Cheers mate! This is amazing, I'm online and surfing. I can e-mail anyone, anywhere. Safe!'

'Can I have a go?' A fair question I thought, after all the work and effort I've put in.

'Yeah, later.' This is followed by a wide sweeping gesture of his hand which I translate as *get lost*. So selfish. I mean, where would he have been without my technical input and natural intelligence? I resort to my original mission of finding something in the fridge and, with it being a Saturday afternoon, the options are slim. I can't wait until my mum gets back from the supermarket. By then it could all be too late, I may have faded away entirely. I need something now.

It is indeed grim in the fridge. Much as I expected, my worst fears are confirmed. Yoghurt, a quarter of iceberg lettuce branching out into a brown colour all of its own making; some cheese, not sure what kind, probably no longer the brand it was when we first bought it; a scraping of margarine; and three overripe tomatoes cracking open in their desire to be eaten. I think of my dream fridge contents: Pepsi-Max, Snickers – both ice-cream and ordinary; McDonald's cheeseburgers; a mound of fresh pasta with bacon and cheese and real Parmesan, not that dried stuff that looks and tastes like grated puke. I had been hanging on the fridge door for three minutes and still none of these things had materialised. I shut the door slowly, sighing dramatically even though there was no one in the kitchen to witness my misery and hunger.

In the biscuit tin lurk three jaffa cakes. Perhaps I can survive on these until Mum gets back? I bravely reach in and pull one out, lie down on the tiled floor to conserve energy levels and put it into my mouth for four seconds before spitting it out into my hand.

It is stale and soft, not chewy or tantalising as the box promises. I have been cheated. I look at the other two sulking at the bottom of the tin and sadly close the lid. There is no hope. I don't know why I leave them in there to die. I should throw them away but I have the smallest hope that if he ever comes out of his room, e-mail man might fall to the same fate. I fear the end is near, when I hear the front door. Hopefully, it's my mum laden with bags of food. But I am cruelly mistaken.

'Isla? What are you doing here?'

My head is so full of food I have entirely forgotten about Isla. Forgotten about the kiss, too, until I see her, right in front of me as I stand in the hall, my hand holding the front door ajar. Panic sets in. My stomach is doing back-flips and I know it's not the hunger pangs. She is in front of me, on the doorstep I share with Mum and Matthew. They will know. They will be able to tell, just by looking at us, that something has changed. Surely? My mum is behind Isla, struggling with bulging supermarket bags that seem to be cutting off the blood supply to her hands. They're strung out white with savage lines across the palms. Indentations. My mum and Isla are together. Isla has Tesco bags, too. Our Tesco bags. I am confused, and panic is rising.

'I met Isla on the way home and gave her a lift,' my mum explains as she thrusts bags at me and shakes her hands to get the blood circulating.

'I thought I'd help her with the bags,' Isla explains as my mum returns to the car for more. They both finally push past me and go into the kitchen. I am no longer very hungry but feel sort of excited, with a bellyfloppy feeling inside. I take the bags in, shut the front door with my foot and follow the pattern of laughter my mum and Isla have made.

An hour later and we are all eating in the kitchen, not just the usual 'we', but Isla too. She is sat next to Matthew who is talking and talking to her, looking and laughing, Mum is smiling and so is Isla. I think I am too. It is so unexpected. I know it's only a meal but normally it's only school and Dave's Deli and lunch times and the library and going into town, so this, in my house, with my family and the laughter and no arguing or embarrassment, or Matthew taking the piss is . . . all right, really. This must be what normal families are like.

Later, Isla and I go to my room. She's been in my room before, sat at my desk, played CDs and games, eaten microwaved chips and ketchup sandwiches and crept into Matthew's room to watch videos, but all in daylight, all naturally planned and normal. It is nine-thirty in the evening and she has just let my mum ring her parents, who have told my mum that it's OK with them for her to stay the night. We've gone from friends, to kissing, to staying the night – in the box room admittedly but still staying the night. It makes me want to tap my feet and impress her with my house and room and how cool my mum is.

I am really surprised it's happening. She only rang to tell them where Isla is and by the time she's come off the phone it's been decided that Isla is staying the night. My mum's just made up the bed in the little box room and gone back downstairs, leaving us to it, no conversations about trust and rules and expectations. She was a bit quiet, in fact, and gave Isla a hug and a kiss good-night as well as me, which I didn't appreciate happening in front of Isla. I am trying to think of the evening ahead. It's Saturday and I need to entertain Isla. It is totally my responsibility that she has a good time and isn't bored. It's my house so it's up to me to think of things to do. Pressure, but I'd rather have it than not.

ISLA

I thought Sunday would be so boring after being at Luke's for most of the day, so I came home slowly, dreading the shouting an' hard sharp faces I expected to be pulled at me. I felt warmish an' smiley when I thought about how I had managed to stay away, staying out all night and no' a girlie sleepover. I didna want all at school to know about it o'course as they would all presume we were into the whole sex thing, but I would enjoy Hannah's big eyes and questions, which I wouldna answer, obviously. Well, no' until later anyway. When I got in, ma mum was ironing in the kitchen, ma uniform, with more to do piled next to her. I felt more than a wee bit guilty and hoped she hadna worried about me through the night.

'All right there, Mum? Are you wanting a hand now?' I thought the offer would buy me a ticket back into the good books but it didn't get me the smile or the face I was expecting. She turned around and I saw that she didna have the iron in her hand.

'Isla, Isla, Islaaa.'

The three-name thing again. I knew I was in trouble but this sounded worse than trouble. The iron was on its stand an' wasna even plugged in. I looked about the kitchen – no lights on and no smells. It was quarter past seven, dinner should be getting itself ready, an' Hannah should be laying the table, her only chore. So where was she? I sat down at the table for four, opposite ma mum who was folding a green tea towel into smaller an' smaller squares.

She didn't have any lipstick on. Ma mum has lipstick in the drawer by the front door, underneath the mirror, behind the books in the toilet, in her handbag, and an old, nearly worn-down one in the glove compartment of the car. She never keeps gloves in there, but she loves lipstick and is 'naked' without it, apparently. So, now, her lips are pale an' a wee bit chewed I think, an' her hair is whooped up into a ponytail, but a lumpy one, a mess done without a brush, looks like a pineapple on top of her head.

'Isla, be brave now. There's been . . . an accident, an' something has happened.'

As she was talking her head was down an' it was in English but it sounded like she was underwater, an' I couldna quite understand through the bubbles an' the dimmed-down sound of her voice beneath the surface. I wanted to cut in and turn up the volume but I also wanted to turn it off. I didn't want to know this. The tea towel was dropped an' I watched it fall to the floor. Then she got it out quickly, while I was watching the green hit the tiles in a crumpled heap. Distracted.

'Last night, she was crossing the road, from the letterbox, coming back over to the shop. It was dark. He didn't see her. She was knocked over. Hit her head. The impact. By the time the ambulance came. Gone already. Isla?'

All this came in short jumps, and in a low voice borrowed from newsreaders, broken an' bitty an' deep. She was looking at me but I seemed to be inside something, like a goldfish bowl. I could see her, mistily, an' hear her echoing, deep, dulled words, as if they were moved away from me, so I had to strain to hear them.

'Isla. Darlin'. I'm so sorry. I don't know what to say. Your dad's with her now, in the . . . chapel.' She had to keep starting new sentences because she didn't know what to do with the old ones she'd begun. They didn't sound right or fit.

What chapel?

'I've been waiting for you, Isla, to tell you. Do you want to go? Your dad will be back soon. It's just he didn't want to leave her on her own. Scared of the dark still, an' the chapel is d—'

I wasn't quite so far away now and her voice seemed to have been turned up, loud, an' was skating over something. Scared of the dark still?

'I didna know she was afraid of the dark. I thought it was cancer an' you just didna know how to tell us.' Ma voice sounded like a boy's, low and quiet.

'Of course you knew. That's why she had to have the nightlight on, keeping you awake at night.'

What? What nightlight? Nightlight! No, no! Words formed in ma head an' made no sense. Hannah? I thought Gran. I thought Gran, they said, Gran dead. Not . . . No!

'*Hannah?*'

'What? Yes, yes. Who did you— Did you think? Gran? No. No! Isla . . . Hannah. She's . . . She's gone. We didn't tell you last night because— I thought it would be better if we— Isla. Isla! Calm down, sit down!'

I remember moving away, the chair scraping, and me screaming. It started up from somewhere, growing until I could hear it coming out of me and then smothered in ma mum's wet jumper, an' the smell of tea and washing-up liquid an' salt, the taste of wet salt. I didn't know where to sit, so I stood, and then I understood the iron an' the board an' ma mum. She didn't know how to sit and she'd had to, waiting for me, until I came home. She couldna stay with ma dad, she'd had to come home and wait for me, an' leave her, leave Hannah!

'Why?' It was the only word I could actually say, an' really mean, an' have an interest in. It was the only word that could make it through the pounding an' the narrowing of ma throat. There was a noise in ma ears, like a cracking, an' I couldna swallow, an' I was blinking too much, an' trying for too much air an' making noises. I was going to be sick. I couldna make ma body work, an' I didna care. Ma legs melted away, an' I was on the cold tiled floor.

Only hours before, she'd been staring at me, hanging on the lounge-room door, listening, enjoying ma being in trouble, smiling at me, making me hate her, making me angry an' wanting to tease her an' be mysterious about the money an' Luke, an' now she's nine an' she's dead. I'm supposed to go before her; ma Gran an' parents are supposed to go first, an' now she's dead. My sister, an' I didna know. All night an' all day, I didna know, an' then I thought it was Gran an' I didna care as much. She was, is, old an' it made sense an' fitted an' would have been bad, but sensible. Older people do die but not nine-year-olds, not ma sister, not Hannah. She's died, dead.

It was a shock later to learn it was the same day, still. I thought it must be days later but it was still Sunday, dark, an' ma dad had returned an' was waking me. I didna know how I got to bed or how long I'd been asleep but I knew that Hannah had died, that she was gone for all time now, an' I'd missed it all, an' I missed her already. Ma dad didna know what to say, so he just told me small bits in a slow voice, holding ma warm hand, with the rest of me under the duvet, boiling hot, all ma clothes on, an' the whole time me looking across at her bed. It looked too neat an' made, no computer games an' clothes spilling out of it.

It took a while for me to come down all the stairs to the shop an' into the back lounge where people were waiting, more upset than me, an' able to cry an' hug me an' tell me things about her, things I didn't know, places she'd been an' things she'd said. It was as if she wasna Hannah, or ma sister; it was as if they were all talking about someone else.

Her friends – the ones who I'd ignored or scowled

at across our bedroom, sworn at for being in ma way – I wasna to know they'd want to look at me an' talk to me about her, an' say her name, so soon, so loud, without warning me first. An' all this an' cups of tea for their parents, an' ma mum offering them biscuits an' talking, an' someone accidentally laughing in the middle of the room. All of this an' it was still Sunday an' she was still dead. I wasna to know all this would happen an' I couldn't listen or speak. I could only stand. Just.

LUKE

Ten forty-three, Sunday night, and I can't wait anymore, I have to ring her. I can't go round. My mum says there'll be loads of people in their house and I'll be in the way. I've tried to explain who I am. I'm her best friend, her boyfriend. I'm important, I think. She'll want to talk, I think.

My mum told me about Hannah as soon as Isla left our place. Mum had been awake all Saturday night, knowing what was waiting, why it could all wait for Isla until she got home. Giving Isla a night of peace before she'd have to be told. My mum said Mrs Kelman hadn't been ready yet, that they were at the hospital with Hannah, that they wanted to be with her through the night. I don't think they could cope with having to tell Isla, or anyone really.

I tried to run out after Isla, but my mum stopped me and I was glad. I don't know what I would have said. So, now I'm waiting, lying on my bed. I've got the mobile in my hand and I'm still waiting for the right time. But I don't think there will ever be a right time.

I can hear the usual noises. It's a normal Sunday everywhere, even here in our village, no one has stopped. Even my mum is downstairs, putting out the rubbish, and Matthew is on the computer with his music on. It's not going to change for him, nothing will be different. He came in earlier and stood awkwardly in the doorway asking me to say sorry to Isla for him, then he left, walking a bit slower than usual, but that's it for him.

I don't know anyone who has died before and now I always will. I'll always remember Hannah, but only because she's died, dead. I would probably have forgotten her otherwise, but now when I hear that name it'll make me sad and I'll always think of her blonde hair and the grin and the computers, and those things will always go together. I wish I had spoken to her more, given her sweets, stuck up for her when Isla kicked her out of their room, all these things, and I am a hypocrite because I should have done it all anyway. I spent last night worrying what people at school would say about Isla staying at my house, half hoping they would actually find out. I was worrying about what Isla would want to do, what I could get away with in my mum's house with Isla in the room across the hall, wondering if she would expect me to try and sneak into her room, and if I didn't there would be something wrong with me. Now, none of this matters and things will never be the same for her and her family and they won't be the same for us, and I feel so selfish having Isla to myself when she could have been with Hannah, but no one could have expected this, to have known this could happen. It just doesn't, does it? It happens to other people on the news, not real people, not me. Not Isla.

How do I do the next thing, choose the right thing, be in the same room as her mum and dad? How can Isla go to sleep now? All of this is racing through my mind, and it's still the first day and there's so long to go. They will have this for the rest of their lives and count the years and have awful things like anniversaries instead of birthday parties.

I can't put my music on 'cos I feel bad, and I can't go round there but I've got to ring. I can't *not* ring but I don't want to, I won't do it properly. Maybe I should write down some things to say, then if it goes silent I'll be OK. God, what if her mum answers? I can't not say anything, and then what if she won't speak or can't come to the phone? I turn on the phone. I have butterflies and feel really sick. I take in a lungful of air and let it out, slowly hoping it will settle me. I press the right numbers, quickly, so I won't change my mind. This is so hard. I can hear it ringing and all I want to do is put it down.

'Hello.'

Oh God, I think it's her mum.

'Hello. It's Luke. Is Isla there? I mean can I speak to her? Please?' I can't say anything else. I can't sympathise or offer pity or bring it up. I'm only fifteen, what the hell could I say? She would probably be angry if I tried. I hear her pass the phone to Isla.

'Hello Luke.' She sounds painful and squashed up. There's nothing more from her. It's like she's lying down and can't get up and can only speak out of the corner of her mouth.

'Isla. My mum told me not to come round, that you would have lots of people. Do you want me to? Do you want to come here? Or just to talk?' I know I'm offering too much, confusing her with options, but I just want to give her something. To try and help in some way, but what way, how? I can't bring Hannah back and I can't change things and that must be all she wants, all I'd want, and if I can't do that then what is there left to say?

'Hmm. Luke, I can't do it. I have to stay. I wasn't here when she . . . so I don't want to leave now . . . I . . . tomorrow . . . OK? Ring me tomorrow, maybe.' And she puts the phone down.

My legs are in the way and I have sighs and lumps of heaviness trapped inside me. I was useless and rushed. I don't want to be, I want to have the right things to say and do. I mustn't go strange or silent or run out of things to say. I have to be calm and normal and not treat her any differently, I think. I try and imagine how I would feel if Matthew died but I can't really. I can only pretend and that's not the same and it feels stupid to try and work out what it would feel like. It's not a game of let's pretend, and I am cross with myself that I thought I could imagine this thing, this death, a word we have never before had to mention.

How do you talk about it? Are you allowed to say the word 'death'? Oh God, Isla sounded so unusual. But if you don't say 'death' then what do you say?

I can't believe how shocking it is to hear her so tinny and empty, even though I told myself this is how she would sound, how she would be. It's the real thing that's the scariest, not the imagining. I wish someone would tell me things. I need to know when to ring and when to turn up and how to act and what to say. I can still hear the phone, the line's dead. I turn it off and put my head down on the duvet. Lying on my bed, upside-down, looking at the ceiling, I try to work it all out.

ISLA

School is silent for me all week an' I canny stop counting things: the days an' how many hours I've slept on ma own; how many neon hours an' minutes I have been trying to get to sleep; how many pairs of bunched-up patterned socks are in her drawer; how many 'In deepest sympathy' cards are on the mantelpiece; and how many people call round every day. It gives me something to focus on, to stop the sick black feeling, to make me remember to breathe in and out, in and out, all day long. Yesterday, the thirteenth day, the numbers started going down after the funeral, when they were at their highest. When the house was full an' noisy an' busy with everyone talking an' thinking about her. It's called a wake. I don't want to think of waking Hannah up an' I canny think of what else the word could mean. People keep telling me to remember her as she was, bonny, blonde and bubbly. I'm no' quite sure why they tell me this, like I'd no' noticed or forgotten how she was or what she looked like because I haven't seen her for thirteen days.

I forgot people's names at the funeral and they looked hurt, fighting quietly for how close they were to her, or me, or our family. Competition between who knew her best, who was her favourite aunt, or her best friend, or her preferred teacher. So many different ages and voices and accents, all in our tiny lounge an' in the hall an' the toilet, an' the cars parked all over the street on double yellow lines an' no one caring. All the rules are wiped out when someone dies, nothing really matters for a wee bit. I could shout an' scream an' stay out all night an' no' do any homework or wash ma hair or clean ma room an' none of it would matter anymore, 'cos *Hannah's dead*. But I do clean ma room an' somehow I wash ma hair and do things almost on auto pilot. Here I am carrying on and so much has happened that there isn't space in ma head to give it all time or proper thought. There's all the normal daily stuff to do an' it all takes so long now that time just seems to run out an' I fall into bed exhausted, shattered, tired beyond belief but wide awake.

At the wake I had to pass paper plates around an' alcoholic drinks, an' ma mum an' dad no' stopping, in their best dark clothes, rushing an' swishing past me, no time to think an' realise. Luke was by ma side an' in ma room an' held ma hand while I had the hiccups in the chapel. I've heard whispers that I haven't cried yet an' that I'm in shock. Everyone's an expert, telling me stories of their own loss.

'Are you OK?' A strange an' stupid question, to which I could find no answer, spoken by too many people: aunties who aren't ma aunts, friends of ma mum's, Scottish voices again, come too late, saying things to ma mum.

'Such a shame, Beth, that this is how we come doon to see you.'

An' more to ma dad, strong, large battered hands awkwardly positioned on his shoulders, patting an' shaking for too long, an' the watered-down smiles, wrapped in black clothes, new looking an' worn with respect, labels cut off that morning.

I cut out her photo from *The Mercury*. She'd have loved being in it if she was here, but that would sort of defeat the point. I read the information about her more than once an' it sounded strange in ma head that people would now know this about ma sister, look at her photo, feel sad for a minute an' then forget. They would never have thought about her if they hadna seen this. She's a name an' information, a wee statistic now. No' ma sister anymore.

KELMAN, HANNAH,
died on 20 October, 2001, aged nine.
Hannah, daughter of Ian and Elizabeth Kelman,
sister to Isla, will be sadly missed.
Funeral to be held at St Michael's Chapel on
4 November, at 11 o'clock.
The family asks for flowers to be sent to
Thompson & Son.

LUKE

I am counting the days. It's been three months, sixteen days, and it's February already. It's making things easier, like when you're little and you count down to Christmas or your birthday to make it go faster. Isla is obsessed with counting things too, as a measure of how far she's come or what she's achieved without losing it, I guess. I'm aware that she needs help. She asks questions a lot, thinks she's obsessing or being silly and self-indulgent. She doesn't want to get trapped in it all and is really trying to cope with other people and their grief, stuff which they want to share with her, almost to prove their pain is justified, that they aren't exaggerating.

She says it's like a competition but she doesn't have to join in because she lives in the same bedroom and she lives with her mum and dad who have lost Hannah too. Everyone else has just misplaced her but Isla has *lost* her.

I listen because I can. I don't have to say all these

things and think them and feel guilty about all the time I've lost and all the things I'll never be able to take back or change. It's like when I argue with Matthew, or deliberately wind him up, or hold a grudge, I know that in a few hours, or if it's really serious in a few days, I know it'll be forgotten. Isla can't do that, and it makes me think about me and her and families and that I should grow up and sort myself out but then in a few days I know I'll forget 'cos it will be normal for me at home, or later on in my life, nothing has happened that me and my family will always have to remember, no dreadful day to circle on the calendar. We'll be all right, but Isla?

'I just . . . I feel so bad all the time. Y' ken, when you dream you've done something really foul, like getting really drunk an' being sick an' insulting everyone, an' you canny remember what you've said or done but you know there was something, an' you wait all day to see if someone will tell you or stop talking to you. It's embarrassing an' your stomach turns over an' you feel guilty, then you wake up an' for a minute or two you think it's true, then you catch on an' realise it were just a dream. You sigh with relief an' you smile 'cos it's all OK, an' you didna do anything bad an' no one hates you. Well, every day I wake up an' feel awful, but I don't get the relief part, or the smile. It's like I canny quite do the full waking up thing.'

Isla's sat on my bed, pulling her hair viciously through her hands and not looking at me. She cut her hair last week. It looks really bad. Well, it did at first, but her mum made her go to the hairdressers to sort it out, and now it looks less worse, I suppose. I don't think she knows why she did it really, she just sort of hacked it off. She just felt like doing it, she said. I reckon it was to see what would happen, what her mum or dad might say. They've gone really strange, not telling her off anymore, or even telling her what to do. She can do what she wants, when she wants. Well, this lasts for a week and then they go the other way and get really overprotective and try to stop her going out at all. They must be so confused. I know I am.

When we talk about this kind of thing, the Hannah stuff, she doesn't look at me too much 'cos I pull the wrong face. I can't help it, there's sadness and pity on it and I can't wipe them off 'cos it's all so terrible. So if she doesn't look at me she doesn't cry. It's not just her hair being hacked off or all the make-up she's started wearing, it's all of it. It's too much really.

When I was first her friend I thought she would just make me laugh and pass me notes in science and stick up for me, go into town with me, talk for ages on the phone about absolute shit, and go to the cinema and listen to me explain *Star Wars* even though she hates sci-fi. I thought the deal was I sort of looked after her at school and made sure she didn't get into too much trouble, and sort of looked like her boyfriend, without all the relationship argument crap that the rest of our year seemed to be knee-deep in.

We sometimes watch TV programmes together, over the phone, so it's as if we're spending the evening together without overdoing the friendship thing and getting on each other's nerves. It was going great, getting jobs together, talking about A levels and after – what we wanted to do, and the unspoken, the always knowing each other in one form or another. Laughing and laughing at her, with her, loving her humour – a girl who really is funny. Feeling jealous when Matthew really laughed at her little bits of sarcasm. All of this just for us, a platonic but not really a girl-boy relationship, which I've never had before. I hadn't thought about this, though, having to think about death at our age. It hadn't occurred to me that we would ever have the conversations we have now, like this one in the dark with the sound of canned laughter from the telly downstairs burgling its way into the quiet of our conversation. This is the hardest part of all, this friendship stuff, and we both know it. It's hard for her, too, she doesn't want to bore me or depress me, but it's in her head and mine and I care and want to live up to the promise of the laughs and the films and the comedy shows, all the easy bits. I want to do the hard bits, too. It's just that I hadn't expected them, they came so soon.

ISLA

I'm glad we went back to Edinburgh, even just for the summer holidays an' no' for good. Strange that, I thought I would always want to go back, to live there again, ma home, but it didn't feel like home, anymore.

Mum an' Dad didn't think Hannah would want a grave, the word an' thought of it didn't seem to make sense next to the sound of her name. She wasn't grave. We tipped her ashes into the wind an' the sea, the Firth of Forth. Just tipped them out an' watched them float away an' mingle with the surf and spray of the water, just like that. In a whoosh an' whisper, my sister Hannah, all gone.

Dave, ma dad's pal, took us out in his boat. It was raining an' that helped. The colours stay in ma head: the choppy, changing blue beneath the boat; the lighter, thinner, watery sky; murky, navy water everywhere. Now there's no one place I have to go to if I want to talk to her, secretly. I can do it in ma head. I don't want to go to a graveyard an' leave ma sister in there on her own. I think Mum an' Dad thought the same.

We didna really talk about it much. Some days, we didna even mention her name, not once, an' it would feel weird like we were trying too hard, trying to be normal again. Mum an' Dad would whisper in their room or over the washing-up, always late at night when they thought I was asleep – like I could sleep anymore. I would hear concern in their voices, the rise an' fall telling me more than words, and I would remember eavesdropping with Hannah an' I'd miss her for the simple things like that. What I hated most was being an only child now an' having to cope with ma mum and dad on ma own. It had been so much more fun having Hannah to share it all with, even if she did annoy me. I'd have it all back, now, anytime, but I knew it would never be. I'd had ma chance.

Then Year 10 was finished and I couldna get over how odd it all was, going back to Edinburgh, well, home really. I honestly thought it would be like coming home an' would be wonderful an' make me hate Maidstone for taking Hannah away, an' I thought I'd no' be able to stop ma mouth spitting out things like, 'if we'd never moved Hannah would still be alive,' but

I didn't. I hoped the lumpy, heavy feeling an' the new dread of holidays as an only child would dissolve as I touched Scottish soil. But it didn't. It was hard to even get off the plane with the load I couldna stop maself carrying around.

I saw ma friends, the ones I'd dreamed about seeing; went to Princes Street, shopping; talked about everything but Hannah; pretended to buy things but I didn't care about my favourite pop group Oasis anymore. We went to McDonald's an' all I could taste was polystyrene. The bagpipes on the Royal Mile played for American tourists an' no' me. Ma friends tried, but there were new things being talked about an' places new to me, that were now old to them. An' the worst, a new girl who was no longer new had slid neatly into ma slot an' I had to be explained to her. I was the one staying in a bed-and-breakfast an' rooms borrowed from relatives. I didna have ma own bedroom in a house around the corner anymore. I canny know if all of this would have happened if Hannah hadn't died, whether it would have been so prickly an' twisted up in ma head.

It's hard to work out how things would have been if Hannah hadn't died, whether I'd still be caring about the things ma friends are talking about, getting worked up 'cos they'll get to go into dinner first at school now they're in Year 11, an' that Robbie Holly is single again an' playing down the football club with his new band. I canny work out who I was before, an' if it were a very different me to the one I am now. Luke says I've changed but in a slow calm way an' that it is normal an' natural after a member of ma family dying. He actually says these sentences but can't help checking my reaction to see if it's OK to talk like this. Sometimes it is an' sometimes it isn't. Sometimes, I hadna even liked Hannah, yet I get all this sympathy, an' teachers wanting me to come an' talk to them about it, but only in their lunch hour while they half-heartedly mark exercise books, trying to listen but without the time to really do so. They give me pitiful looks when they ask if we have sisters or brothers in the school, so they can avoid sending duplicate letters to the same home. As if I care about the school's photocopying budget.

I get hugs from strangers, friends of ma parents, an' more money, an' no being told when to go to bed, an' no real arguments anymore. Ma dad offers me more freedom one day, then snatches it back the next, constantly jiggling about with the balance which he canny seem to master. Now a father of only one, he has too much time for me an' doesna know how to measure it out properly. Ma mum sits on the edge of her bed in the dark, crying with her mouth wide open an' tears streaming down her face, but making no noise despite the racking great sobs which are silent, but deadly.

Sometimes, I'd wanted Hannah to go away so I could be an only child, to have ma own room an' no little ghost following me around, eavesdropping on ma conversations with Luke, listening outside the bedroom door with two of her wee friends an' then falling to the floor in fits of giggles when I suddenly flung the door open.

She used to annoy me so much. I remember telling her one time on the way to Cornwall that Mum an' Dad were murderers. I said they were taking us to a smuggler's cave an' were going to kill us an' hide our bodies, an' that no one would ever suspect 'cos they were our mum an' dad! The poor thing believed me, but then she would. I was her older sister an' what I said was gospel, for a few years anyway, till she got wise. I feel awful now, but that's what older sisters do isn't it? That's what I miss, having a little sister to tease. Never thought I'd say it. Didna think I'd have to.

Luke's been grand, much better than ma best

friends who've known me an' Hannah all our lives. Luke practically lives around ma house, taking up some of the space left in ma room by Hannah's absence. I never thought the room would ever look big to me.

LUKE

Isla looks up at me where I'm sat on Hannah's bed, which is OK now, but wasn't at first. I'm listening to her. I'm getting better at discussion, this talking stuff.

'Y' ken when you're wee an' small or . . . when you're in science an' you've lost the will to live an' you're staring at something on the floor, or out the window – it doesn't matter what – an' you're dreaming but awake an' you think about the future an' wonder where you'll be an' what you'll be an' . . . an' even who you might be with?'

'Yes . . . and you sort of go into a gorm, you know, like you're gormless and can't stop staring and your eyes are on pause. Yeah, what about it?' I answer, pausing to check my comments have made sense to both of us, and wait for her to continue.

'Well . . . what do you think about?' She wants to hear my voice, not to hear her own. She's been trying to turn her voice off lately, to give her brain a break.

'Um . . . jobs.'

I wasn't really expecting this and haven't thought about me. I like to think about things before having to commit myself to commenting. I try to master the fine art of talking and thinking at the same time, which Isla seems to have had private lessons in and has definitely graduated with honours.

I actually think girls are programmed at birth with talking skills and discussion techniques. I've learned some stuff from my mum and, of course, the God of chat shows and pouring our hearts out on TV, Jerry Springer, but what Isla is going through I have had no training in. Chat shows tend to steer clear of people who say 'My nine-year-old sister was hit by a car and died'. They tend to go more for, 'I am a fifty-year-old woman whose husband is having an affair with my brother's wife's sister's next-door neighbour's cousin, and also I am having a sex change!'

I decide to have a go at making it up as I go along. I choose the seemingly safe topic of the future.

'Umm, like what job I'll be doing. I think the RAF if I get an A in maths and stats, and I quite like Maidstone but I want to go places you know . . . um . . . and I want my mum to have someone, not to be on her own 'cos Matthew'll be going to university and then there'll be only Mum and me, and I don't want to just leave her and that to be it. I want her to have some fun and someone to look after her. Umm, I'd like loads of money and CDs and a Audi TT coup—'

I stop my list and look at Isla to see if I've been rambling and so I can stop myself talking about my mum too much. Don't want to overdo the Ricki Lake sentimentality thing and go all American on her. We've started doing this lately, wandering into sketchy conversations about things that we've only recently started thinking about. I think it's got something to do with the exams being mentioned every millisecond at school. Up until now things have worked out OK. School's always just been there and teachers give us a timetable and patronise us by checking we are where we should be, but it's always been OK because we won't have to sort ourselves out for ages yet. Until now, in Year 11, it looms dangerously – 'it' being the *after* life, after school, when you presumably get a life. Although it is a classified secret, and if I told anyone I would have to kill them, I did actually listen to what Miss Hughes was saying in PSHE the other day. It was about CVs and interviews, and I started counting and even considered using my year planner, previously untouched and missing in action, since Year 7. Apparently you can get a new one every year but I never bothered using the first one so there didn't seem much point asking for more.

I can't believe it's nearly the end of school and revision and exams in less than six months. I feel like I've been in school for ever. I suppose I have really, since I was four or five. It seems strange to think that my life will change lots just because I'm sixteen and the law says I can do what I want. Not sure I know what I want, or where and how to do it, but that's all we've been dreaming about since the start of Year 10, and now it's nearly here I wish I had another year to go.

It's like the summer holidays. They turn up and seem to stretch ahead into infinity, then suddenly they're over and you wish you had just one more week, one more and you'd be ready to go back to school. But the truth is, it's never going to be enough, you're never going to be ready, so you just have to jump to it and hope it will all work out OK and it will, probably. I feel really different thinking in this order, almost grown up – almost.

ISLA

We've got a carol concert at school an' it's no' the thing to want to be in it but I really like singing an' Christmas. I'm going to go for it, although I'll tell the others I've to do it as part of ma music coursework. Double that with an order from Mr Mitchell who you don't argue with an' I should get away with it an' dodge the sticky labels of 'keener' an' 'square' an' all the other cruel catchphrases our school seems to be bursting with, a new one every week. Half the time the teachers canny understand our words. We did a lesson on it in English – accents an' dialects an' slang – an' it wasna too bad – a wee bit interesting actually.

I'd no money to buy presents but last Saturday Luke and I went into town, to window shop. Just to check out what was there, making sure everything we wanted in HMV last week was still there, an' still just as expensive an' out of our reach. So, we took the bus into town, getting on for half fare by lying about our age, an' gaining a wee feeling of superiority over the bus driver, our common enemy. He sits in his cubicle, refusing to give any change an' views everyone under twenty with deep suspicion. He hates me an' Luke 'cos we never have our bus passes on us. When Luke tried to get on with Matthew's old pass on Wednesday, he went mental, shouting at us with words like 'imposter' and 'fraud'. I think the power's gone to his balding head. Ma dad calls people like him a 'jobsworth', like all they have in their life is their job. Traffic wardens are another. Dad refuses to believe they're human an' reckons the government grow them in a laboratory somewhere to develop a hatred of the human race. Sadists I think he said when he got his last parking fine. I think that might have had something to do with it!

Unfortunately, our school driver 'captains' (as he calls it) the Saturday buses into town and Luke's mum was busy private tutoring in their kitchen. Fifteen pounds an hour, Luke told me. Ma parents were of course working in the shop. They work all the time now so they don't have to sit down to a table with an empty space for Hannah; so they don't have to see the fridge blank without her latest drawings; so they don't have to miss telling her to put her glasses on to watch the TV. Ma mum checks things with me now, like if I have money for lunch an' that I'm getting enough sleep, an' no' trying to cope with too much, an' still refusing to cry. She wants me to cry, says it's healthy an' a release, an' that I shouldna 'bottle things up' – her favourite saying lately. She's been going to the doctors a bit less and has come off the tranquillisers that I am not supposed to know about, the ones no one mentions. She still has a load of awful self-help books lying around the house though, almost like a replacement for the pills. She quotes from them at the worst times. Just when things seem to be going OK for a bit she tries to talk to me or ma dad. It sends ma dad mad. Lots of things seem to send ma dad mad at the moment. Maybe he should have had some pills too!

I feel the same as ma dad, though. I don't want to help maself or get in touch with ma feelings, let alone ma inner child, for God's sake! I entirely mean to bottle things up, very firmly, an' I don't care that Mum wants me to cry. I canny help it, I'm so scared that if I start, if I let out a tear or noise that isn't controlled, an' stop holding in ma stomach an' ribs an' heart, if I let it go I'll never get it back an' everything will literally spill over, pour out of me. I don't want to gush, to dribble an' drip all over ma mum's shoulder and smother her with tears an' snot. So I keep quiet, until it's night, when I try to lie down in the same room, the room that is now just mine. I didna think I would ever long for someone else to be in it with me, especially no' Hannah. I think that's why I have the nightmares, that someone is there, because I want so badly for her to be there again. As ma eyes get heavy I try an' make out the little hump of duvet that she used to make, an' I listen for the little noises of sleep an' breathing through her nose, the mouth resolutely closed so that no spiders could get in. She once did a project at school an' was horrified an' outraged to discover that humans eat eight spiders in their lifetime, whilst innocently sleeping. Refusing to consume her quota of eight, Hannah vowed to us at dinner one night never to leave her mouth an open invitation to any spider, ever. She got her wish.

So, on Saturdays, if I wanted out of the house, which I did, we had no option but to get the bus. Luke wasn't that into the shopping or the early carols, or the queues or the gaudy lights an' decorations. Maybe in a week or two when it was actually December, he might get more in the mood. I noticed now that it was me cheering him up an' watching for the rare smiles from him, rather than the other way around. I was worried he might be getting a wee bit impatient with me. I'm no' the most experienced person an' I think he thinks I am. Thinking about Luke an' kissing an' his body an' whether he would put up with me, made me realise that I was coping. Only four weeks till Christmas, my second without Hannah, but I was coping. I am coping.

LUKE

I knew the novelty would wear off. Admittedly, I didn't think it would take this long but patience is obviously a virtue. Matthew is back down the pub, having abandoned his room and provided me with the opportunity to use his new computer – the reward for my patient vigilance. I've got Isla's e-mail address at the Post Office but I don't think her dad would be too impressed if I used it, plus it wouldn't be very private – not that I've got loads of private things to say to her. It's all very platonic and lacking in any details. Still, we've moved on since the first kiss and followed it up with many more superior and now practised kisses. I know her bra size. She's decided my thighs are the best bit of me. We've banged elbows, heads, and feet whilst trying to manoeuvre on her small, single bed, propped against sloping ceilings and a variety of other assault courses we have to get over. So, we've not got very far. The whole thing has been made more difficult than it would normally have been. I mean

Hannah dying has changed everything in Isla's life, and I want to be there for her and to understand. I have needs though and I'm normal. She's beautiful and I can't help but want to be with her, but I respect the fact that she's got things on her mind other than that. I understand really, but bloody hell! So respect, respect is good. To take my mind off sex, women, and mostly Isla, I turn on the screen and make the Internet connection and eventually, when it's down-loaded, I surf. Nothing of interest, definitely don't want a chat room, or to shop or make friends – you always sound like a total loser. Matthew's personal files on Microsoft Exchange look much more enticing and not even in code. Practically giving me his consent. Some essays for media studies – oh interest! E-mail from Natwest, bank details, not very detailed as Matthew doesn't have much money and then I see my surname, his surname, listed over and over, but not our initials.

a.field@line2.net	16/10/2001	Hello Matthew
a.field@line2.net	29/11/2001	Re: last conversation
a.field@line2.net	03/1/2002	Re: news!
a.field@line2.net	14/2/2002	More details
a.field@line2.net	19/5/2002	Re: Information

| a.field@line2.net | 28/7/2002 | Exciting news! |
| a.field@line2.net | 12/12/2002 | See you soon |

The last one only a few days ago. My *dad*, his name and obviously his e-mail address. I click on it and words appear. I see 'Dear Matt' over and over. I skim-read the letters: 'work is improving', 'How's college, your mum and Luke?' Then later, information in what must be a reply to Matthew's questions about a Claire and the word 'engagement', which in the last one has become 'wife'.

My head is churning and too much information in the form of neat black letters and symbols is circulating in my head. My hands are gripping the edges of the desk and the screen is now the only light in Matthew's room. I feel ten years old. Like lots of events have taken place and I've been evicted and excluded and sent to my room to contemplate Lego and Matchbox toy cars. Too many pieces are missing and all this time he's been creeping into our home, through the computer, and Matthew let him, keeping it all a secret in his computer. Sharing his life and our lives. Why couldn't I write to him? Why didn't Matthew tell me? A new wife? Mum! I mean they've been divorced for seven years now. A new wife for him? Matthew and me will be stepsons. Who is she anyway, this Claire?

What about Mum and the money and all of that, and Matthew's been talking to him and keeping it all to himself. I don't close the file or turn off the computer. It's become secondary to this revelation. I leave Matthew's navy-blue-lit room with the words of love from my dad, for *him*, pounding in my head.

ISLA

Two Saturdays after the painful an' unrequited shopping trip to which we subjected ourselves we went back for more. This time to try an' actually buy our reduced families something, both of us with just two wee presents to buy, both wishing we'd one more person to buy for. Luke didn't seem to care which shop I pulled him into or where we were going for lunch, obviously no' Dave's Belly. We like to try out new places all the time an' have pretty much covered Maidstone now. It was Luke's turn and he chose with a flippant an' casual air the Internet Café. I hate computers an' the Internet, although I'd no' admit it to anyone I canny use it. Even Hannah knows how to— I mean *knew*, but I canny get used to the past tense: 'she did' rather than 'she does', takes some getting used to. They teach it in primary school now, the Internet, an' here's me at fifteen no' knowing any more than Windows an' Encarta. So I bit ma tongue an' followed him in as he seemed set an', well, it was a new place.

It was very busy. Lots of older people, college an' university students, an' scary waitresses who scowled at everyone, all of them wearing khaki drawstring skirts an' wee silver vest tops an' spiky ponytails. I canny wear a spiky ponytail as I had a disastrous razored haircut last month an' there's no sign yet of the twenty different layers, which I now have, growing back. So Luke guides us to a wee rickety, stainless steel table an' looks around the room, scanning.

'Who're you trying to avoid?' I am concerned an' curious, mostly curious.

'You see Matthew anywhere?'

He hasna taken in what I said. I search the room for Matthew.

'No. Why? Have you two had a fight?' Luke was beginning to annoy me. He'd been really evasive, no' listening lately, no' finishing sentences, an' leaving ma questions answered.

'No we haven't. Yet.' Luke was bubbling with anger an' his eyes were screwed up, like the sun had hurt them.

'Luke, what?' I needed to know. I was worried because he looked so twitchy an' guilty.

'Matthew's been talking to my dad, and he's getting

married.' He spat it out, then looked away, folding his arms across his chest as if it was all nothing to do with him.

'Who to? Luke? Who's he getting married to?' I was guessing it was Luke's dad an' no' Matthew getting married. I was guessing quite a lot.

'I don't know.'

He had no information an' I needed more.

'How come? Does Matthew know who she is?' I shouldna have asked but I hadn't thought ahead to what answer Luke might give.

'Matthew knows everything. He and my dad get on really well; he doesn't need to talk to me. So if you want to know anything you'd better ask Matthew.'

I was so slow. Of course Luke wouldn't know because he's too proud to ask or to talk to his dad himself.

'Did you hear them? Talking?' I tried it softer this time.

'No. I found it on the computer. They've been writing, sending—'

The waitress, silver and khaki, pen an' notepad in hand, tutted impatiently beside us. Luke stopped an' looked to me for help.

'Two Pepsis and two chips?' I suggested, an' he

shrugged with a 'whatever'. The waitress looked unimpressed with our inexpensive, an' predictable choice. I looked around the room an' saw croissants, brioche, bagels, pain au chocolate, ciabatta, an' other interesting words plastering the walls in wavy, sloping italic writing. I felt lacking in style an' grace but Luke was more important than ma stomach an' ma street cred.

'E-mail? Did you tell Matthew you found them? Or your mum?' Many awkward things slid untidily into place.

Luke shook his head, only his hair moving as he studied intently the hard, cold table.

'Are you going to? Is that why we're in here?' In the Internet Café! He must have brought the address with him and it would have been a waste not to, an' I couldna stop maself, I had to suggest it.

'Why don't you e-mail him? If Matthew has it must be all right. He might want to speak with you but is a wee bit nervous because of the money, an' your mum, an' all that there.'

I had run out. Luke was smiling though. I was so relieved.

'Yeah. I know. But I feel so grim. I'm really nervous. What if he doesn't want to speak to me? I mean he could have asked Matthew.'

He stopped. I was rolling ma eyes.

'He's probably nervous. You've got the address an' it's an e-mail, so it's no' like the phone where you could clam up. It's no' face to face, so you can take it slow.'

Our uninspired chips an' Pepsis arrived, an' the waitress's lip curled with distaste as she deposited our bowls. Why we needed chips in a bowl instead of on a plate I don't know. I looked at Luke an' he snorted. We were obviously no' cosmopolitan enough. God knows what they would have done if they knew I canny actually use the Internet an' still don't know how to send an e-mail. I'd probably be evicted an' barred for life.

LUKE

I know I should bring it up somehow but I was hurt at first and felt totally left out. I should tell her before she finds out. I honestly haven't got the words for it though. I haven't done this kind of thing before, talked to my mum, broken something to her, needed her to sit down, and it's strange and cold to me. Matthew should be doing it, doing his job, he's older. I don't want to upset her, and what if she cries? What if she's still in love with him? Davey's dad remarried two and a half years ago and his mum cut off her hair, loads of it, cut it into a short bob thing feathered with layers cut into it, and had sunbeds and started going out more. I don't want my mum to hack off her hair. I don't think she loves my dad anymore but then I wouldn't know, she's hardly likely to confide in me.

I'm sat waiting. On the verge of returning to the sanctuary and comfort of my room. If she doesn't come in by the third jaffa cake and I make it to my room in less than twenty steps, including the stairs, then I can stay up there and leave it, for a better time. I'm taking my second step, whilst swallowing the sponge bit of the jaffa, when French books burst into the kitchen, piled up to her chin, and a big brown bag and a smaller navy handbag are thrown on to the table. Too late.

'Hello. Hungry? I got a cooked chicken from Tesco on the way home, so if you can hang on?'

She lays her hand on my head, then grimaces, removing her now wax-coated hand and rubbing it on a tea towel before taking the chicken out of its foil packet and putting it in the oven. I thought it was cooked. She puts pans full of potatoes and peas and water on the hob, fills the kettle and puts two teabags into two flowery mugs, managing to smile and crack jokes she'd heard at school – all this at the same time. I can only do one thing at a time in the kitchen or have to fear for my life and the lives of those around me. Mrs Cowper our home economics teacher says I have no coordination or sense of timing. Mum takes off her shoes and stirs the tea. I hate tea, especially Earl Grey, but I drink it to keep her company, and if I have some chocolate in my mouth at the same time it's bearable. She sits down at the table and passes me the sports section from her paper. I check the scores absentmindedly, while working out the appropriate words in my head. I've obviously been staring because she asks, 'What?'

'You know e-mail?' A poor cowardly start, I know.

'I have observed it.' Dripping with sarcasm, whilst watching me over her second mug of tea and *The Times*.

'Well, Matthew, right, he's sort of been e-mailing Dad. Letters and news, and I've read them. By accident.' I shove in my denial of involvement and show solidarity with her all over my face.

Mum sips her tea. It burns her tongue and that takes the blame for her swear words which are nothing to do with the temperature of her Earl Grey.

'Oh, so what kind of . . . what did—? How is he? Tom – your Dad?' She says his name lumpily, as if it's invaded her mouth, shoving it out with her tongue.

'Married.' It seems short and sharp but not as shrill or shocking as her laugh. She cackles, a real crack-up of a laugh, and puts her mug, which has been hiding her face, down on the table, spilling it. 'Oh, my God! Who to?'

She's smiling and laughing, and is definitely not in love, unless she's in denial, but I think it's OK.

'I don't know. He mentioned a Claire lots so it must

be her, Matthew'll know, seeing as he's the chosen son.' I can't help my voice rising up at the end like I've got the taste of a lemon trapped in my mouth. I know it'll make my mum feel sorry for me and quickly surround me with perfumed words and arms and a kiss, but I sort of want it, a bit.

'Luke, you know your dad loves you. He's probably been e-mailing Matthew because he's got a computer. He'll want to talk to you too, lovely. Come on Luke, you know that.'

She's still smiling, and holding both my hands awkwardly across the table. She pulls my eyes back up from their focal point on the table and makes me half smile. I know she's making sense but I still feel funny. I'm furious with Matthew for not telling me about it.

'Try not to be cross with Matthew. He would have told you. He knows you're still angry about the maintenance payments, but don't be, Luke. The solicitors sorted it all out months ago. Luke, don't be cross, please. I'm not. Were you worried about *me*?'

Mum is sorting me out. I was supposed to be helping her, to be selecting the right phrases and tones of voice and stopping her from crying. She's laughing, hugging me, then is dealing with the chicken and plates and moving French books out of the way – teachers!

ISLA

I finally had to master e-mail an' overcome ma fear of technology an' computers an' all things that beep loudly and embarrass you every time you make a mistake, which can be quite often if you're no' a computer sci-fi geek, whiz-kid type person, which I am no'.

Luke wanted to e-mail his dad an' needed company an' back-up as it's no' safe alone in the Internet Café unless you're armed with age or go to university or wear silver. As we matched none of the obvious requirements we were nervous an' edgy in there but knew better this time when it came to ordering. Cappuccinos and croissants rolled off our tongues on to the waiter's pad an' fifteen minutes later into our stomachs. We were in! I had no one to send an e-mail to, so I helped Luke by pointing out his typo errors every couple of words, but I think this may have annoyed him more than it helped.

'Isla, it's not an essay, OK, it's only my dad and if he can't take a few spelling mistakes . . .'

His outburst trailed off into the coffee scented air. I looked around the café an' wished Hannah was around so I could describe it to her in detail when I got home, exaggerating the bitchiness of the waitresses an' the gorgeousness of the Italian looking waiters. That's what I missed, the telling stories part an' seeming glamorous an' grown-up in ma world where I went out at night to exciting places that she would have to wait years to go to. Ma parents definitely weren't impressed by ma outings to the cinema, or occasionally to parties where the highlight was drinking large quantities of a foul concoction called 'punch'. In reality, it was an empty Coke bottle filled with a variety of some parents' drinks cabinet, the end result of which was more than one person making friends with the toilet bowl or a hedge and swearing 'never again'.

This had been both me an' Luke, an' it had given us a matching set of hangovers as presents for Christmas Day, which made the awkwardness of the day itself all the worse for me. I didn't really enjoy playing 'let's pretend everything is all right', an' invite loads of family down. They only came because of Hannah. Instead of using the usual excuse of the six-hour journey, they came feeling that, in the light of our loss, it would be too rude not to.

So, of course, to get drunk the night before Christmas was clearly the only thing to do an' make a total arse of maself in front of half ma year an', more importantly, Luke. Though he was quite busy himself, doing a macho routine of downing shots of tequila, no' aware of the fact that I'd lost the power an' control over ma legs an' couldna stop the trees an' sky from spinning violently round ma head. It's no' something that either of us particularly wants to repeat but there's no doubt we will, according to Matthew who took us home an' sorted us out with pints of water, glasses of a fizzing liquid called Resolve, none of which really helped ma throbbing head but it was sweet of him all the same. Matthew says everyone says 'never again' the first time they get trolleyed, as he put it, an' that you soon forget. Well, I won't. I still feel sick if I even catch a whiff of ma mum an' dad's red wine, an' those Coke bottles in the shop no longer look as innocent an' welcoming as they used to.

LUKE

When I went on work experience I had no idea that I would have to do so much work. None of the teachers told me I would have to behave *all* day, and answer the phone and try to work out really quickly the answers to all the questions people ask. They expect you to know about everything, just because you're wearing a tie and shirt, are a bit tall and could maybe be an adult. I have done a week which went really slowly. I suppose this week will be better as the manageress has gone on holiday, leaving just me and Janine out the front, with the rest of them in the back offices. I don't know the names of the others as they don't seem to think I am worthy of being spoken to. Janine speaks to me though and asks me to make her coffee, while she tackles vital tasks such as sorting out her nails. I know what she's doing but I kind of like her so it's OK. She calls me cute and ruffles my hair which is annoying 'cos then I worry that it looks a state but don't want to check it in front of her.

I have to wear ties and white shirts and smart trousers and no trainers, obviously. Matthew takes the piss out of me every morning as he crawls out of bed and hauls the nearest T-shirt over his greasy-haired head – or so he'd like everyone to think. But I know for a fact that he chooses what he's going to wear to college the night before and carefully manufactures the 'just got out of bed and I am soooo cool that I don't worry about what I look like' look. So he can get lost.

I don't want to get a job in The Kitchen Company but I do like the stuff I am doing. My dad got me the job, which I only took because it was that or work in the Spar corner shop. I was definitely *not* going to have all my mates coming in there from school trying to make me sell them beer and cigarettes; plus, the man who runs it thinks I am eighteen, or pretends to so I can get served in there.

So I let Matthew sort out this placement with my dad. He's never in this office as he works in the other branch in Leigh-on-Sea, which is safely miles away. Everyone knows I am his son though. He turned up on my first day and put his hand on my shoulder and told everyone to treat me as if I were just anyone on work experience, so that was a painful and hideous experience for everyone concerned. He is so embarrassing and doesn't get it that he can't do that after months of me not seeing him. He can't just suddenly come in and clap his lumpy big hand on my shoulder. He was talking really loudly to me, so that everyone would hear, saying he's my dad and how lucky I am that he got me this work experience. I suppose he's all right but I hate his new wife. She's so annoying and ignores me totally, like I am part of something my dad did before, something best forgotten which was probably some silly mistake he'd made. She's got stupid curly hair and glasses and a crap name and I cannot see at all why he would want to be with her.

Isla reckons she's OK and that I would hate *anyone* my dad got it together with. And that's another thing, the thought of my dad getting it together with someone, it's disgusting. For some reason, if he'd stayed with my mum I would never have thought about this and I would have just presumed – once, very quickly – that maybe they had sex once or twice a year but only if they had to. But now he's married again I am suddenly realising that as newlyweds they must be having sex lots, that my dad has sex, and a sex life, and I . . . well, I . . . don't. It is very shocking and new, and something I can't think about too much for the safety of my head which can only cope with so much of this stuff before it combusts.

ISLA

When she said two months, in maths, I couldna believe it. I mean it were only Christmas a wee while ago, an' then there were the mocks. No' that we took those seriously, 'cos they're just a trial run, aren't they, an' you say you won't revise for them 'cos the real exams will come along later, an' you'll revise for those instead. An' now it's nearly exam time again, except this time it's no' Year 11 mocks, it's the real bloody thing an' I've to admit I'm scared, an' nervous.

I haven't really revised, apart from maths, as I canny do that at all and there's some who do an extra maths GCSE called stats, 'cos they're so good at it. Can you imagine doing extra maths? I've problems with what I'm given and I am in Set Three but I don't care as long as I get ma C grade an' can be a nurse, I think.

I did it a bit on work experience in Maidstone General but I wasna allowed to do much as I had no insurance. Apparently you're no' allowed to go higher than six inches off the ground in case you fall or hurt yourself an' your parents want to sue the school or hospital or whatever company you are with. Anyway, I ended up wiping puss off a man's leg an' I thought I would say something about how disgusting it was but he just lay there looking so grateful an' sad all at the same time that I just smiled at him an' told him what he'd missed in *EastEnders* whilst he'd been asleep. Old people sleep a lot, and really like telly and telling you what they're to eat that day. They've to choose their meals, all of them, each morning. I canny cope with more than toast in the morning, never mind deciding what I want to eat for ma lunch an' tea the rest of the day. I think they find it something to look forward to, an activity sort of. I canny imagine being old or frail like ma Gran or the man in the hospital. It seems like I've got so long to go yet, which is kinda nice.

I think I will pass ma maths. Luke's been doing past papers with me. Ma dad tried but we just ended up having blazing rows every Sunday morning. He resented it 'cos he should be in the shop helping ma mum with the papers an' that. I hated it, an' sometimes him, 'cos I don't get maths and know I will never need to work out the length of the hypotenuse in a triangle or whatever it is. I want to know how to measure things like how much water or blood or medicine I need to give someone, or how much change I should have from a fiver, an' things like that, not the trigonometry lark that I canny get ma head round.

So, every Sunday, although I do ma best to talk Luke out of it an' persuade him otherwise, he tries patiently to show me how to do long division and work out the square root of something. If there has been a match the day before or he's missed *Match of the Day* I fill him in on what Gary Lineker has said an' can lead him away from figures an' calculators for a wee while, even resorting to ma worst Alan Hansen impression, frantic eyebrow action an' the nasal voice, which only just works because I'm Scottish. This lasts until he catches on to ma game an' that's it, I've had it, an' he turns into Mr Field, maths geek, shaking his head when I attempt to distract him away with kisses, refusing to let me break his will power. I think he gets that from his mum.

I'm a wee bit worried about what will happen when school is over, we go on study leave in May an' it's no' that far away now. I mean, most of us will go on to Maidstone College but it won't be the same. We won't be in tutor groups anymore an' there'll be lots of new people an' older, mature students – they call them OWLS, for Older Wiser Learner Students or something. Luke might be going to another college or even to do RAF training an' that's what scares me most. He thinks it'll be fine wherever he goes, an' that we'll be fine. We don't seem able to talk about it. We sort of float around the black box we have stamped, 'DO NOT TOUCH' an' manage to avoid the issue magnificently.

LUKE

I am totally broke, strapped for cash, completely Trebor mint – cockney rhyming slang for skint, as I have to keep explaining to Isla who doesn't quite get cockney. Not that I'm doing the whole *Lock, Stock and Two Smoking Barrels* and giving out the 'I am a cockney geezer, rough-diamond, East-End-boy' vibes, just because I live down this end of the country. There were some diamond geezers at the Leigh-on-Sea office of my dad's company and they did sound quite cool. I only went there twice, just to be polite and to see him when he invited me. Matthew said I was going whether I liked it or not, as he had borrowed Ripper's Mini and had gone to the great trouble of skiving off college, an experience and concept clearly never undertaken before. I felt obliged.

It was so much easier with Matthew there. I wish I was like him, although I would rather stand naked in the middle of town than admit that to him. His perfectly coiffured head is inflated enough with his predicted A-level results. He is so laid back, calm and funny, he knows just what to say and has started shaking hands with men and even dipping his head to kiss women on the cheek when he meets them. I mean, when did he learn to do that? And who told him it was OK? And it most definitely was. All the women smiled and turned their cheeks to him with what appeared to be pleasure, and all the men shook his hand firmly and said, 'All right mate?' I just stood behind him and nodded my head at people. My dad was smiling and saying, 'These are my sons, Matthew, and Luke.' It felt like he added my name at the end just in time.

Sometimes, Dad scares me and other times I think I scare him for some reason, like he's feeling guilty or bad about something. I keep waiting for him to tell me Claire is pregnant. That would be the worst, if he had another baby. I know he's always wanted a girl. That would be too weird, a stepsister. I have only just got used to the whole stepmum deal, and it's not just her, it's her mum and dad and her brother and his kids, who are all my step-cousins and step-grandparents and stuff, I suppose, if you can be bothered to work out everyone's titles and how we are all dodgily related.

Matthew just calls them all by their first names, including Claire. I don't call Claire anything, and definitely not *Mum*. I just sort of talk to her without using her name. I've got away with it so far this evening. Matthew accepted the kind offer of going back to Dad's new flat to have a Chinese takeaway with him, and Claire of course. Clearly, she can't cook, unlike Mum who at least tries. So I have to behave and try not be the brat Claire obviously thinks I am. I am determined to be like Matthew, except I'll leave wide open spaces between us, so I don't have to see her too closely or smell the sickly Dewberry perfume she smothers herself in and everyone else she is in close contact with.

My dad has been watching me all day, looking at me carefully, with a variety of expressions on his face which have ranged from surprise to anger to pride, I think. I wish he'd pack it in, it makes me look at the floor to encourage my fringe to flop down, so no one can see my eyes, so no one will know what I am really thinking. I agree totally with the Japanese – or is it the Chinese? – who refuse to be photographed as it will steal their soul. Well, I don't want my dad or her to look at or try to read my eyes too much – they'll see and know what I'm thinking. I bet this is what the dinner is in aid of. She's probably pregnant and they've summoned me and Matt here to break the happy news to us. I wish they'd get on with it so I could go home, instead of being in this flat which is too small for my dad. He looks like he's come into the wrong house. It's all cream and beige and minimalist or distressed-effect DIY or something crap like that. It is so feminine, it's got to be her flat and taste, and he's just gone along with it.

He's really different here. He drinks red wine and reads *The Guardian* and watches lots of films, which they talk about a lot. Discussion they call it. We didn't even have a telly in our house, for years. He always read, with Mum, sometimes sharing the same book and laughing and reading bits out to one another. Quoting. Claire tries again to pull me in by name dropping. Well, she can cast her line away, I am not biting.

'Did you see it, Luke?'

I can't stand her even saying my name. I know it's ridiculous but it feels strange and she is basically a stranger and if I keep my head down and don't get a picture of her in my mind, with her red painted nails on my dad's thigh, then she can remain a stranger. I dimly recognise that I have to answer her questions.

'What?' This is as much as I can give. Yet she tries again.

'The new *Star Wars* film, the film we've been discussing for the last ten minutes.'

That word again, why can't she just say *talking about*. She's such a show-off and a name dropper, she'll probably tell us she knows the director or one of the main actors. She's still staring. I'm not going to get away without a reply. I can feel Matthew glaring at me, even though I am not going to look up at him.

'Yeah, it was crap.'

I actually thought it was OK. Not as good as the first one, but I like what the director's done and how he waited until he had enough money to afford the special effects. Not sure about Ewan McGregor's accent, though. I did think it was watchable and an interesting new way to make a film, but I certainly wasn't going to share any of this with her.

I chance a quick look up from the IKEA perfect pine table I have been focusing my gaze on for the last hour. She is still staring. Will this woman never give up? Finally, she does and follows my dad out to the galley kitchen. The flat is so small you can't fit a proper kitchen in it. They love that, giggling in the kitchen like . . . like I don't know what, but it hurts my stomach. Matthew grips this opportunity and my arm, quite firmly.

'Luke, stop being a pain in the arse. She's actually all right and you can see he's happy. Stop acting like a spoilt brat or I'll tell Mum.'

The last bit nearly makes me laugh, it's so ridiculous, and Matthew starts to smile, which helps my smile on and I take a sip of the Fosters beer she's poured for me. I love Fosters. Dad must have told her to buy it. I know I should do a Matthew and be graceful and witty, an adult basically. I just don't want to. They are both strangers and it's hard work and it's all jumpy and I don't know how to act around them and I keep waiting for the pregnancy bombshell, as if I want it to explode so I'll have something to react against and shout about 'cos, as yet, I don't suppose they've actually done anything wrong. It just feels like they have.

I mostly make sure I'm in the same room as her, Claire, like tonight. She always looks at me when I talk to her, like when she just asked me if I wanted another Fosters, grabbing on to the fact that I have accepted her beer with delight and that for the first time this evening I am smiling. If I do this, smile every now and then but without looking at her too much, then it might be all right. I'll just make sure I only speak to her when she is looking at me, or next to me, which unfortunately for me seems to be a lot of the time, as if she likes me or something perverse. I don't have to use her name though. I don't have to acknowledge her as my dad's wife, as someone with a name, which I suppose is Mrs Field, the same as Mum's. Now I have started this rule, this refusal to use her name, I can't stop. No one's noticed though, so I think it's OK.

ISLA

Ma dad wanted me to work in the shop yesterday, Sunday, even though I'd worked most of ma summer holidays so far. There was no way I was gonna be in there on ma own all day, so I dragged Luke in to help me an' he didna mind as we were getting paid for our trouble, plus, Sundays usually make us feel suicidal. Luke says they're longer than any other day of the week and devised solely to punish us with hangovers and menace us with the threat of work the next day. Sometimes, he is so melodramatic but in a funny way. He does it to entertain me. He's been working with his dad a bit.

It's no' bad having finished school, even though I am going back, even if it's no' to Stoneley High, it's still all part of the same thing really. I like being a semi-adult though. Sixteen, nearly seventeen, well, next year anyway. Y'can do lots at ma age now. I can buy cigarettes, sell them in ma dad's shop, drive a tractor, an' there's one more thing, not that I want to smoke or drive a tractor but just knowing I can if I want to is . . . good. The other thing is I can get married if I want, and leave home. I told Luke this on ma birthday a couple of months ago an' he looked a wee bit concerned and fell over his words and explanations as to why none of those things would be a good idea. I found it annoying at the time that he'd the cheek to presume that I was after marrying him!

'Don't flatter yourself. I'm no' saying I want to get married and no' to you. I was just listing ma rights as a woman.' At this he laughed an' looked relieved all at the same time. I think I might be a bit of a challenge for him at times.

'Right, I mean, not that I wouldn't want to marry you, Isla. It's just that I want to go into the RAF and I haven't got any money and your dad would have me kneecapped, so— what?'

The scowling I had started with, turned into laughter, as his crumpled frown unravelled itself all over the top of his head. Then, once the laughter an' smiles had settled in the shop an' placed a warm, glowy feeling around us both, I decided to open all the windows, turn all the heating off, fling the door wide open an' let in the snow, wind an' hail with ma shattering-of-the-warmth question:

'Luke . . . do you think we'll last an' stay together, especially if you are going off an' no' coming with me to the college?'

Before I had the time to check maself or read through the scripted version of this conversation – which I had painstakingly worked out so that I would say all the right things an' discuss it all in a mature adult manner – I had unleashed a scrambled-egg mess of ma thoughts all over Luke's alarmed face. This was the taboo subject – not as in a bottle of alcohol, of which we had by now managed to overcome our temporary hatred. This was the box containing the taboo subject which we had silently agreed no' to open until we had to. Apparently, I had chosen this moment, with the shop full of customers, to ask Luke about the dreaded 'f' word. The *future*. Our future, an' more to the point whether we had one. I kinda hoped we did, though I'd no' want to admit it to Luke, as I thought it might scare him off, an' I didna want to seem clingy an' desperate. Looking at Luke's face, I think I was already there, renamed in his mind the official Queen of Clingy an' Desperate, an' was left on ma own wearing the crown of the title as Luke had gone out the back on the pretext of getting more cigarettes, even though I'd just restocked the shelves.

LUKE

I want to be clear in my mind but until I get my GCSE results how can I know where I am going to be and what I am going to be doing? I wish people would stop bloody hassling me and asking me what my plans are for after school. What A levels do I want to do? Have I considered what profession I want to go into? Where am I going to base myself? What's my five-year plan? Five-year plan! I don't know what I'm doing in the next five days, for God's sake. Then there's my mum. Matthew is going to get good grades, of course, then he'll be off to university and it'll be just me and Mum. My dad has asked me to go and stay with them over the summer. I don't know what he wants. It can't be for me to live with him. Even though they haven't told me Claire is pregnant, I am still waiting and expecting it. I don't trust my dad but I do like where he lives. It's more exciting than here and I have to admit, only to myself, that it might be OK in the new flat, and I'd get to go to all the West End premieres courtesy of Claire, but Mum—

Mum isn't a loner or anything but she works too hard and doesn't have time to go swimming anymore, now she's Head of Languages. I'm not sure she even wanted the promotion but apparently you are supposed to go for these things in teaching, before you get past it and some younger teacher steals your position. She is happy, I think. I don't ask her but she smiles and laughs and doesn't mind that Dad has remarried. She even talked to him on the phone two weeks ago, when they were sorting out who was going to take Matthew up to university. He's going to Warwick. He had to get at least two As and a B, I think. Anyway, he got three As and a B. I don't know how, as he hardly did any work and devoted his revision time to worshipping at the altar of the PlayStation. He must be a natural genius and a lucky sod. I would have gone to Oxford or London, with three As and a B, but he reckons the course at Warwick is what he wants to do. Nothing to do with the fact that Ripper is going there, too, or at least to an old polytechnic nearby, but we don't mention that. Ripper is doing film studies, which I can't help but feel jealous about. What a way to spend the next three years, watching films and then talking about them. He assures me it is 'so much more than that, Luke' and will be 'incredibly challenging and taxing on one's brain'.

Yeah, right.

So, I know that when I have finished my A levels and sign up for my seven-year contract with the RAF that she, Mum, will be OK, but I still feel guilty. Then, of course, there's Isla. I know we're only sixteen and that but I really like her, but that's it – *like*. I don't think I love her, but I've never been in love so how would I know if what I feel is? I can't stay out here in the stockroom any longer. I've been procrastinating for a week now, carefully skirting around the issue, whilst trying to control the butterflies in my stomach every time I see her or the phone rings late at night and I know it can only be her. The shop sounds noisy and full again and I know she's out there waiting for my answer, same place, same question, same time, a week later, still waiting.

'I got some more *Cosmopolitan* and *The Net*. Looking a bit low there.' A complete lie as Isla just restocked the racks, but I don't know how to begin. I take the plunge, again hoping for inspiration from the women's magazines I am flicking through. However,

'Is he the one?' and 'Is your man faithful? Take this test . . .' aren't providing me with the guidance I'm looking for. I go it alone without the prop of *Cosmo* and *Company* which we are both disinterestedly riffling through.

'Isla, put those down for a minute. Look . . . I'm probably going to do my A levels, at Maidstone College, but after that I am . . . probably going to sign up with the RAF for . . . seven years, probably but . . .' After overusing the word probably I run out of steam and other words to move and reassure her. My head adopts a downwards position until she comes over from behind the counter – leaving three people queuing, coins clutched in their impatient hands – and kisses me, full on the lips, in front of everyone. He shoots, he scores! Jackpot! Obviously, somehow through the muddle of words and mumbling and downward head movements, I have managed to say the right thing, have made her day and have been rewarded for my trouble. Unfortunately for me, at this heralded moment Mr Kelman chooses to walk into the shop, back from the Cash and Carry, which tends to make him psychotic on the best of days, but coming back to find his daughter in my arms, her lips firmly attached to mine, and observed by the majority of the customers whose faces are arranged in a variety of disapproving expressions, bodes badly for me. I mentally practise charging past him to leg it out of the shop and possibly out of the county – make that the *country*. However, Isla has other plans and maintains a vice like grip on my now shaking arm.

It's not that I am afraid of Mr Kelman. I'm bloody terrified. I know he likes me as much as a father can like his only daughter's boyfriend, especially one who has unfortunately brought her home drunk once or twice, who has got her into trouble once (or twice) at school, and who he suspects of sleeping with her. So, his liking for me doesn't really stretch much beyond the door no longer being slammed in my face when I come around to call. Occasionally, I will receive a grunt or even a hello but that is as far as the courtesy reaches. Mrs Kelman, however, loves me, I think it fair to say. Evidently, Mr Kelman isn't entirely relaxed about his wife's preference for me as a potential son-in-law. So, facing him now, I am glad there are witnesses in the shop as he questions me, somewhat volubly.

'What are y'doing? Am I no' paying y'to run ma shop? I'm sure there were no mention o'kissin' ma daughter and providing the village with entertainment . . . ! I'm waiting.'

I hope he will wait long enough for me to get my passport. Painfully, I recognise that the waiting period will not last long enough, and brave the wrath of Kelman.

'I'm sorry Mr Kelman, we were just making up, we've had a bit of a row but everything is sorted now and I'll finish here.'

I place the counter between us and quickly serve the crowd that has gathered by the till, hoping to show willing and avoid a scene. Isla, however, has other plans.

'Dad! A word upstairs, please . . . now.'

It never fails to impress me how a few words from Isla, a five-foot-three midget really, can transform this giant to a small and obedient boy. He actually turns around and follows her up to the flat where what can only be described as noise starts up, accompanied by thumping, and then silence. I find the silence the most disturbing as I give people their change and try to concentrate on working out their weekly paper bills as they enjoy the entertainment floating downstairs into the shop.

We don't really argue much in our house, not shouting, not this tense rowing, but then we haven't lost anyone in our family. I think that's what is at the heart of it. Mr Kelman doesn't want to lose another daughter and is therefore tyrannically overprotective of Isla. Not that he undervalued her when Hannah was alive but things have, well, changed. Irrevocably. Isla is constantly trying to adjust the balance and living on a seesaw in the meantime. And I thought I had troubles.

ISLA

Part of me wants t'meet new people an' make new friends, an' to start ma biology course an' work with bodies an' scalpels an' slides, conducting experiments in labs, but if I canny tell Luke about it all an' sit opposite him in the refectory with MTV on in the background, providing endless celebrities to criticise an' analyse, then I'm no' sure. I try an' convince maself that I will meet new boys an' that I may even find one or two of them attractive. What more could I want? I have been waiting for college for two years now, counting the minutes on the absurd white school clocks, waiting for the time when I could choose what I wanted t'study an' could rid maself of maths and French, which weighed so heavily around ma neck, like a millstone.

But the boys at college won't find me attractive – not a funny-looking Scottish lass, with a temper and a thing, a loss, grieving still. Luke understands an' I don't want to have t'explain it all to a wee new person, an' why I might be sad every now an' then. But I don't want t'be this sad thing that tells him what to do, an' I don't want him to have conversations with his mum about his feeling he has to be there for me. I know he feels guilty that he might leave me on ma own an' I wouldna be able to cope, but I would. I would pretend everything were fine, that I were happy with ma new lot, that the very word 'new' was no problem for the likes of me. I would be hard an' tough an' resilient an' cope on ma own an' make maself meet new people an' stop seeing everything as 'new' an' therefore scary. We talked about it on his bed, in the dark so we wouldna have to arrange our faces into the right expressions, an' could be honest. We could only do it in the dark, with the music on in the background, in case we went silent an' caved in under the seriousness an' depth of it all.

'Do you want to go to Maidstone College? You don't have to just because everyone else is y'know.' I thought the words 'everyone else' would make it sound more objective than if I said 'I am'. I didn't really know how I'd done with this as I couldna see his face.

'I do want to go there. It's just the contract with the RAF. If I sign up, I sign for seven years and that starts straight after my A levels, and I just want to be sure. I know how you feel, that you're worried about stuff.'

Luke's favourite noun is *stuff*. It covers everything he finds difficult to talk about. I try another approach.

'How do you feel about us? Is it just a school thing? Are we . . . just good friends?'

I nearly shoved in a 'I don't care' on the end but I couldna manage to force it out as I were concentrating so hard on ma breathing, an' trying to see his reaction in the dark. I was tempted to turn on the wee side light but that would reveal ma concern, painted brightly on ma face.

'I care very much for you! Of course we're not just friends. I mean we are friends but we're all the rest as well. God! I thought you'd have realised that by now. Do you think I have this with all my female friends? Why do you have to have so much, like, reassurance? Why can't we just keep having fun and carry on as we are? You know how I feel about you. I've never met anyone like you. God! Why do you complicate everything with stuff?'

I knew it was a mistake. Luke only asks questions when he's angry. Normally, he's too worried about what the answers may be to ask awkward questions. I'd been pushing him, trying t'make him explode so he wouldna be so tightly wrapped up all the time. I had no idea why I wanted things to change. I didn't have anyone to talk it over with an' it had been going round an' round in ma head for weeks now, ever since we chose our AS options for college. I wanted him to tell me for once how he felt about me an' no' to avoid it an' say, 'We're fine aren't we?' an' things like that. No matter what he says to appease me, things will change when he leaves an' goes off to train an' he'll meet new people, an' so will I even though I don't want to an' it won't work but I know I canny keep him here. I know anyone I told, especially ma parents, would say things about our age an' how young we are. They say that already.

All that doesna have anything to do with how jumpy an' sick an' nervous I feel. I don't care what he says, all this complicates things. At least, it does for me. Maybe that's because I am so new to it all. The thought of everything I have, an' know, an' am familiar with, changing an' getting swished up into the past, terrifies me. An' once it's in the past, then Luke will no longer be ma future.

'Isla? Try not to think about things so much, OK? I won't let things change between us, I promise. Even if I do go away, you will still be the same person and so will I. We'll still feel the same way about one another won't we? All right? Now come here . . .'

I'm shocked at how completely I disagree with him. As he pulls me easily into a hug I know I canny make him see what I see, an' feel what I feel. I smile at him, even though he canny see me in the dark. I can see him in front of me through ma memory. I trace the outline of his face an' take in his smell, inches from my lips, from my face. This will be what I remember. Even if things don't work out an' he doesna come to ma college I will always have his smile an' the kiss an' the conviction an' loveliness of his words which insist that we won't change an' that all will be fine. I will have this hope to comfort me, even though I dread the reality an' cynicism that is waiting for me in the back of my head, ready to invade the present. I have Luke's hands holding mine, softly stroking the palm of ma hand, an' his smile, an' the nod, an' the kiss which says it'll be all right, an' it will be, probably.